camp
CONFIDENTIAL

Winter Games

GROSSET & DUNLAP
Published by the Penguin Group
Penguin Group (USA) Inc., 375 Hudson Street,
New York, New York 10014, U.S.A.
Penguin Group (Canada), 90 Eglinton Avenue East, Suite 700, Toronto,
Ontario, Canada M4P 2Y3
(a division of Pearson Penguin Canada Inc.)
Penguin Books Ltd, 80 Strand, London WC2R ORL, England
Penguin Ireland, 25 St Stephen's Green, Dublin 2, Ireland
(a division of Penguin Books Ltd)
Penguin Group (Australia), 250 Camberwell Road, Camberwell,
Victoria 3124, Australia (a division of Pearson Australia Group Pty Ltd)
Penguin Books India Pvt Ltd, 11 Community Centre,
Panchsheel Park, New Delhi - 110 017, India
Penguin Group (NZ), Cnr Airborne and Rosedale Roads, Albany, Auckland
1310, New Zealand (a division of Pearson New Zealand Ltd)
Penguin Books (South Africa) (Pty) Ltd, 24 Sturdee Avenue, Rosebank,
Johannesburg 2196, South Africa

Penguin Books Ltd, Registered Offices:
80 Strand, London WC2R ORL, England

Cover design by Ching N. Chan

Front cover image © Vicky Kasala/Photodisc Red/Getty Images

Text copyright © 2006 by Grosset & Dunlap. All rights reserved. Published
by Grosset & Dunlap, a division of Penguin Young Readers Group, 345
Hudson Street, New York, New York 10014. GROSSET & DUNLAP is a
trademark of Penguin Group (USA) Inc. Printed in the U.S.A.

Library of Congress Control Number: 2006019981

ISBN 0-448-44392-9   10 9 8 7 6 5 4 3 2 1

camp CONFIDENTIAL

Winter Games

by Melissa J. Morgan

Grosset & Dunlap

chapter
ONE

Posted by: Tori
Subject: Sunny SoCali

Hiya Lakeview gal pals,

It's January and I'm staring out the window at the bright LA sunshine, wishing you were all here with me to enjoy it! Don't hate me, but it's sixty degrees out today. I heard about the big storm that just blew through NJ and NY, so I figured I'd check in with you to make sure you weren't buried under ten feet of snow. Believe it or not, I wish I got to see snow more often out here. So, what's new with you guys? Write back ASAP. I miss you all!

Love,
Tori

Tori sighed, took one more glance out the window, and reluctantly fixed her gaze on her computer, where her e-mail was up and running. Her Camp Lakeview friends would say that she was so lucky if they saw this beautiful weather. In truth, Tori felt anything *but* lucky today.

The cursor on the screen blinked at her, waiting, but the words Tori knew she had to write just wouldn't come. She was supposed to be sending out an Evite for the ski weekend her parents had told her she could have up in Lake Tahoe over Presidents' Day weekend, but instead, she was turning into the Queen of Procrastination.

The list of the five names she'd chosen was sitting next to her keyboard, but the longer she looked at it, the more horrible it seemed. Jenna, Alyssa, Nat, Grace, and Sarah—the only girls she was going to invite on the trip. She'd tried to pick the five girls she knew the best from Camp Lakeview, but also the five girls who would match up the best for the long weekend. Nat and Alyssa were inseparable, and Tori'd gotten along great with Jenna, Nat, and Grace all summer long. On top of that, Jenna was loads of fun, always pulling pranks and kidding around. And Sarah was Miss Athletic, but not as obsessed about it as Alex, so Tori figured she'd catch on to skiing right away and would be able to help the other girls learn.

Some of the other Lakeview girls wouldn't have worked out nearly as well for the trip. Chelsea, for instance, was a total downer, always whining and bossing everyone else around. Karen was sweet, but she was too quiet. And Priya spent so much time with her best friend, Jordan, that Tori felt uncomfortable asking her to come skiing without him. But what about Brynn? And Valerie? And Alex? Tori wasn't as close to them, but they'd all been nice to her over the summer. And Alex and Jenna were great friends, and so were

Brynn and Grace. How could she ask Jenna without asking Alex? Or Grace without Brynn? Every time she thought she'd picked the right five girls, heaps of doubt crowded into her brain. There was no way she could possibly send out this Evite.

Tori gave her computer one final glare and headed for the gym, where she knew her parents were playing their daily game of squash.

Maybe there was still the teeny, tiniest chance that her parents would change their minds. It was worth one last shot.

Her dad had had the glass-enclosed gym built as a rooftop addition to their house. Tori's parents were into juice bars and fitness, but Tori had only used the gym a handful of times (and that was when she had her friends over for Pilates). When she got to the top of the gym stairs, she found her parents prepping for the sauna.

"How was your game?" Tori asked.

Her mom grinned. "I'm reigning champion."

"And I'm the resident sulker," her dad added.

Tori laughed. "That's okay, Dad. You can still beat me any day."

"Coming from someone who never plays, I'm not sure that's a compliment." Her dad smiled. "And to what do we owe this unexpected visit? You never come up here, sweetie. What's going on?"

Tori took a deep breath and dove right in. "I wanted to talk to you about the ski trip." She turned on her best doe-eyed, pleading daughter face. "Isn't there any way I can invite more of my friends? I know you said only five girls tops, but we can rent another condo so more can come. I'll even help pay for it with my savings."

Her mom shook her head. "The money in your savings is for college. You know that."

Tori chanced another look at her dad, but he wasn't budging either. "Sweetheart, we've been over this before. Our condo only sleeps seven comfortably, and two girls are already going to have to share a bed."

"They can bring sleeping bags," Tori started, "and extra pillows. Or sleep on the couch with blankets. The couch is big and—"

Her dad held up his hand before she could say anything else. "We agreed that we'd pay for the lift tickets, ski rentals, and food for five of your friends. I'm sorry, Tori, but the decision's final."

Tori bit her lip. "But I can't choose between my friends like this. It's just not fair."

Her mom kissed her forehead. "Honey, I know it's a tough decision for you, but if your friends are as nice as you say they are, they're going to understand. And tough choices like this are all part of growing up."

"And if all else fails," her dad added, "you can blame this on your evil parents. We'll take the fall."

"It's not that simple," Tori said, but she could see that her parents had made up their minds. She was stuck with their decision, awful as it was. "I'm going to the beach with Michael this afternoon," she said, sighing as she turned away. "I'll have my cell if you need me."

Tori had met Michael a few months ago, and for a while, they'd been like a regular Romeo and Juliet. Michael was the son of one of Tori's dad's clients, so at first her dad had forbidden her to date him. Eventually, though, her dad came around, and now Tori could see Michael whenever she wanted, without all the Shakespearean drama (although sneaking around *had* been kind of fun).

But now, even spending the afternoon with him didn't do anything to improve Tori's mood. She sat in the warm sand, watching Michael skim the waves on his surfboard, but all she could think about was the ski trip. She barely even noticed when Michael sat down next to her, until he nudged her playfully, shaking a few drops of salty water onto her.

"Still zoning out about your friends, huh?" he said.

Tori nodded. "I can't cancel the whole trip just because I can't invite everyone. But the girls I'm not inviting are going to hate me forever."

"Hey, nobody could hate you." He smiled. "It's just not possible. But maybe your other friends could pay their own way? If they rented a condo on their own, your parents couldn't say much, could they?"

"No," Tori said, "but that'll never happen. The girls that I'm inviting already have to pay for their plane tickets out here, and that can get pretty pricey. There's no way everyone else could afford plane tickets, food, lift tickets, rentals, *and* a condo. Even if they split it, nobody our age has that kind of money."

"So what are you going to tell the girls you're

not inviting?" Michael asked. "I mean, you can't just keep it a secret for the next month, can you?"

A knot the size of a watermelon tightened in Tori's stomach. The thought *had* crossed her mind. A secret wouldn't be as bad as lying, would it? Tori sighed and rubbed her forehead. This whole thing was giving her one massive headache. "I don't know what I'm going to tell them. But no matter what, it won't be fun. We might as well cancel our movie plans for tomorrow, because I'll be busy getting killed by my former friends."

Michael laughed. "There won't be any killing. Yelling, maybe, but no killing."

"Thanks for that vote of confidence," Tori said, laughing a little. "Maybe I'll just change my name and move out of the country if that happens."

"But not before the movie tomorrow," said Michael.

"Not one second before." Tori smiled.

"And in the meantime," Michael said, "how about coming for a little water ride with me?" He nodded to his surfboard.

"The Pacific Ocean in January?" Tori asked. "No thanks. You have a wet suit. I don't."

"A walk, then?" Michael tried again, holding out his hand.

"Now that I can handle." Tori grinned.

That night, after she'd said good-bye to Michael, Tori sat back down at her computer to fill out the Evite for the trip. She'd felt better after the beach, but now her heart was pounding with fear all over again. As she started typing, she knew one thing for certain. If making decisions like this was part of "growing up," as her mom had said, then she didn't want any part of it. No way.

▲ ▲ ▲

"Sarah!" Abby yelled from the bottom of the stairs. "Are you coming sometime in the next millennium, or am I going to have to go to the batting cages without you?"

Sarah giggled as she pulled her light brown hair into a ponytail and grabbed her softball bat and glove from her bedroom closet. Abby could be *soooo* impatient sometimes, especially when sports were involved. Like right now, for example. Even though softball season wouldn't start for another three and a half months, and there was no chance of practicing outside in the bitter New England snows they'd been having, Abby insisted that they go to the indoor batting cages every Sunday afternoon to keep from getting rusty.

Sarah stuck her head out the bedroom door and saw Abby pacing at the bottom of the stairs. "I'm almost ready!" she said. "Why don't you come up here for a minute? I promised Alex and Brynn I'd fill them in on my date with David last night." David was the first guy Sarah had ever really liked. In the past, she'd usually wanted to beat up boys instead of hold their hands, but that had changed over the summer when she met David. He lived in Vermont, so she didn't get to see him very often, but his dad had come to Boston on a business trip this weekend and brought David along with him. It had been great to see him, and she couldn't help wanting to spill the details. "How about I check my e-mail superfast right now," Sarah called down to Abby, "and then I'll tell the girls that the date went great, and that I'll fill them in on the whole story later. Deal?"

Abby gave Sarah a very exaggerated frown. "All right," she said finally, climbing the stairs. "As long as I don't have to hear about how he held your hand in the movie theater for the whole show. You've told me ten times already. And we get to stay at the batting cages for an extra fifteen minutes."

Sarah grinned. "You got it."

Sarah and Abby went to the same middle school in Stowbridge, a tiny town just outside of Boston. Last summer at Lakeview was the first time Sarah had really gotten to know Abby, and even though they'd gotten off to a rocky start, by the end of camp they were great friends.

Sarah knew how important their softball training was to Abby, so she made sure to keep her e-mail to the girls short, promising details later. But just as she was about to disconnect, a new message popped up:

Ski Weekend! You're Invited!
Host: Tori
When: Presidents' Day weekend, February 16–19
Where: Lake Tahoe

It's time to hit the slopes, Lakeview Ladies! My parents have a fab condo that's right off the lifts at Squaw

Valley, and they're footing the bill for food, lift tickets, ski rentals, and lessons. All you need to do is buy your plane ticket, and you're set. I can't wait to see you!

Will you attend? ____Yes   _____No

Sarah practically screamed with excitement, a huge smile spreading across her face. Going skiing with Abby and all the other girls from Camp Lakeview would be such a blast. She'd never been skiing before, and even though she and Abby had thrown around the idea of going up to Vermont for a weekend, she'd heard that East Coast skiing couldn't even come close to West Coast skiing. The West Coast had dibs on sunshiny weather, perfect powder, and gorgeous snowcapped mountains. This ski trip had her name written all over it.

"Why do you look like you just won the lotto?" Abby asked, peering at Sarah's ecstatic face.

"Oh, wait till you hear this," Sarah started, ready to share the good news. Abby would be totally psyched, and the two of them could start planning for the trip together.

But just as she was about to read the whole Evite out loud, a nagging sensation made Sarah skim over the invite list. And there it was, plain as day: Jenna, Alyssa, Nat, Grace, and Sarah. No Abby, and no Alex, Brynn, Priya, or Valerie, either. Could that be a mistake? Maybe the Evite got screwed up and left some of the girls off the list. She'd have to check with Tori. But in the meantime, what was she going to tell Abby?

"Earth to Sarah," Abby said, laughing and

waving a hand in front of Sarah's face. "So? What's the big news?"

"Um," Sarah stalled, clicking the Evite closed and quickly skimming through her other e-mails for another piece of news. There was an e-mail from Nat, and as soon as Sarah read it, she knew it was perfect to share with Abby.

"Guess what?" she said, trying to match the enthusiastic tone she'd had before. "Nat's up in Connecticut right now visiting her cousins, and she's going to see Simon today! She hasn't seen him in a few months."

"That's it?" Abby said, deflated. "*That's* the big news? Yeesh, I thought you were going to tell me something super-exciting."

"Well, it's exciting for Nat," Sarah said, feeling completely stupid. "It's great, you know, that she's getting to see him and everything."

Abby grinned and shook her head. "Yeah, it is. I'm happy for her. But *now* can we go hit some balls?"

"Sure," Sarah said, slipping on her coat and gloves. As they walked to the neighborhood rec center, Sarah reminded herself to e-mail Tori to get the scoop on the trip later. She was sure this was all a mix-up, and that Abby and the other girls would be invited as soon as it was all straightened out. But in the meantime, a persistent guilt settled down inside her for a nice, long stay. Not because she was on the Evite list and Abby wasn't, but because she'd just lied to one of her very best friends for the first time ever. And no matter how many ways she rationalized it, it didn't feel right at all.

chapter

TWO

Nat pulled her scarf tight and dipped her hat further down on her forehead. It was freezing on the waterfront—her feet were completely numb, even inside her boots, and the wind was blowing in from the ocean like a hurricane could be coming any second. Of course, this type of weather was nothing unusual for January, but why, of all places, had Simon wanted to meet her at Mystic Seaport in the dead of winter? Nat could see how the quaint town of Mystic, Connecticut, with its adorable little antique shops and historic buildings, would be great for summertime touring. But tramping around in sleet was not Nat's idea of a good time, even if she was getting to see Simon for the first time since November.

Speaking of Simon, where was he, anyway? Nat peered through the window of the tiny diner he'd popped into, but she couldn't make out anything through the rain-streaked glass. He'd said that he would only be gone for a minute, but that was at least ten minutes ago. For the first time since Nat had met Simon at camp two summers ago, she was annoyed with him. Well, maybe not really annoyed with *him*, but more like annoyed with the way this weekend was turning out. And she couldn't even explain why.

She'd been so excited about seeing Simon. Her aunt and her two cousins had dropped her off in Mystic while they went shopping so that she could spend Sunday afternoon with him before her bus ride back home to Manhattan. But now that she'd been with him for the last few hours, she just couldn't understand why she felt so . . . so out of sorts.

"I'm back," Simon said, appearing by her side with a big grin on his face. "Sorry that took longer than I thought, but here you go." He held up a paper plate, soggy with grease and overflowing with deep-fried . . . something—Nat wasn't sure what. "It's a seaport specialty. Fish-and-chips. Try one. You'll love it."

Nat glued a smile to her face and willed her nose not to crinkle at the smell of the oil that glistened on each strip of fish. Sushi was her thing . . . not this acne case waiting to happen. She cautiously picked up a piece of fish and, after giving herself a millisecond pep talk, took a big bite.

"Mmm," she said, trying her best to swallow. "Good."

Simon watched her closely, and his smile wilted. "That's okay, Nat," he said, shrugging. "You don't have to fake it. I can tell you don't really like it."

Nat took a deep breath. "It's just that Mom and I tend to stick to mostly organic stuff."

Had Simon just forgotten about her obsession with sushi, or was it really possible that after a year and a half of knowing each other, he didn't know that about her? It wasn't his fault, she reminded herself. During the school year, they hardly ever got to spend time together, unless Simon came down to New York to visit his friend Rick who lived there, or if Nat came up to Connecticut to visit Trish and Vicki, her cousins. At first, the long-distance thing hadn't bugged her at all, but the last couple of months had been different. She'd made a lot of new friends at school this year, and met some nice guys, too, and she was finding it harder and harder to fit Simon into her social circle. Simon had hung out with Nat's friends Hannah, Bryce, Mel, and Gretchen a few times when he visited, but he hadn't really clicked with them.

Her friends were into Manhattan culture big-time, and so was she. She loved discovering new shops in the East Village, trying the latest specials at Sushi Samba, and going to as many discount shows as her allowance would permit. But once she'd taken Simon to see a black-light puppet show and caught him snoring halfway through, so she knew he wasn't as into the metropolitan lifestyle as she was. In fact, she was starting to worry that they might not have as much in common as she'd originally thought.

Simon slipped his hand into hers, and they stepped out from under the shop awning into the rain again. Nat caught Simon glancing over at her a few times, and once he even opened his mouth like he was going to say something, but then he closed it again. She struggled to find something to say, too, which was a first for her.

"So," Simon said, "how are your parents?"

Nat stopped herself from laughing just in time. How were her parents? That sounded like something her mom would say at a dinner party, not something that would ever come out of Simon's mouth.

They needed a change of subject, and fast. But just as Nat opened her mouth, a big truck drove by, sending a tidal wave of frigid, muddy gutter water over her and Simon. Nat screamed, trying to brush the brown water from her face and hair. Her jacket, scarf, and jeans were dripping, and looking over at Simon, she saw that he wasn't in any better shape. His curly black hair was matted down with the dirty water.

"Oh my gosh, Nat," he said. "I'm so sorry. I should've seen that truck coming."

Nat laughed through chattering teeth. "It's not your fault. There was nothing you could do." She tried to wring some of the water out of her scarf.

Simon started to run down the street. "I'll be right back," he said. "I'm going to get some paper towels from the diner."

"Simon, wait," Nat said, catching up to him. "You know what? Even if the towels soak up some of the water, our clothes are going to take forever to dry in this weather. Maybe," she paused, debating her next words, but secretly wanting to say them. "Maybe I should just call my aunt and go home."

Simon sighed, staring at the ground, but slowly he nodded. "Yeah, that's probably a good idea."

After her aunt picked her up and she'd gone back to their house to pack and change out of her drenched clothes, Nat gave her cousins the rundown of the whole afternoon.

"It was awful," she told them as she finished drying her hair.

"Define awful," Vicki said, putting the plastic bag holding Nat's wet clothes into her weekend bag.

"Nothing to talk about, long moments of awkward silence, uber-processed fish, and gutter water," Nat said.

"That's definitely awful," Trish agreed, giggling a little until Nat glared at her. "Sorry."

"What am I going to do?" Nat asked. "I miss Simon when I'm not around him, but being around him isn't really working so great."

"I don't know," Vicki said, "but I *do* know you're going to miss your bus home if we don't get going."

"I guess I don't have to think about this right now," Nat said as they took her stuff downstairs to load the car.

But after she'd said good-bye to her aunt and cousins, and the New York bus had pulled away from the station and onto the freeway, it was all Nat could think about. She needed a venting session in the worst way, so she rummaged through her bag and pulled out the BlackBerry her dad had gotten her for her birthday. Since her dad was always traveling for film shoots, he thought it would be a great way for the two of them to stay in touch. But it was also the perfect way for Nat to stay in touch with Alyssa, Jenna, and all of her other friends from Camp Lakeview.

She logged onto the blog that Andie and Becky, the counselors from 4A and 4C, had started for the girls from both bunks, and posted a message asking for guy advice. Then she added a quick note about the camp reunion: "I know we have no idea when it will be yet, but since it's always in NY, I wanted to invite you guys to crash at my place for the weekend again, just like last year. Everyone from both bunks can come, but it's BYOSB (Bring Your Own Sleeping Bag). It'll be so much fun!"

When Nat refreshed the page, a message from Jenna appeared on the screen.

Posted by: Jenna
Subject: Tori's ski trip

Hey girls!
I just got Tori's Evite for the ski trip and I'm totally psyched. I already checked tickets on CheapFlightz, and they're running a Presidents' Day special. The fares are *soooo* cheap. I'm going to buy my ticket tonight. I'm totally ready to hit the slopes! Woo-hoo! Write back soon and let me know if you're all coming.
TTYL,
Jenna

Nat's heart skipped a beat. Ski trip . . . *what* ski trip? She hurriedly logged off the blog and into her e-mail. Phew . . . there it was—an Evite from Tori for a trip to Tahoe. In a month! Suddenly Nat's worries about her date with Simon washed away. What perfect timing. Nat needed to see Alyssa and the rest of her Lakeview friends more than anything right now. Maybe she had enough money saved from her weekly dog-walking job to pay for the plane ticket, too. She made a quick phone call to her mom, who said she could go as long as she paid her own way, and then she got on IM to see who else might be going.

<NatalieNYC>: hey girls! anyone home?

<BrynnWins>: Nat! How r u?

<SoccerLover>: I'm here, too.

<BrynnWins>: Hey, Alex!

<Alyssa11>: Me three. Nat, how was ur weekend in CT? Give us the details on Simon . . . now!

<NatalieNYC>: (sigh) things didn't go that great.

<BrynnWins>: ?

<NatalieNYC>: i'll explain l8tr. long story. did u see jenna's blog post?

<SoccerLover>: Yup. But I didn't get an Evite.

<BrynnWins>: Me neither.

<Alyssa11>: I got one. But, um . . . I don't think Jenna checked the Evite before she posted that note. Here's the thing. It looks like Jenna, Nat, Grace, Sarah, and I are the only ones on the invite list.

<NatalieNYC>: no way!! that has to be a mistake.

<BrynnWins>: I hope so. It'd be such a bummer for us all not to be together.

<SoccerLover>: Well, we'll be together for the reunion, whenever it is. Nat, count me in for the weekend at your place. I wouldn't miss it!

<BrynnWins>: Me too.

<Alyssa11>: I'm in. But let's figure out this thing

with the ski trip, too, k?

<SoccerLover>: Definitely. I can't imagine Tori leaving anyone out on purpose. And I LUV to ski!!

<NatalieNYC>: i'll e-mail her right now and see what she says. ttyl.

<Alyssa11>: Bye

Nat logged off IM and wrote a quick e-mail to Tori about the trip, explaining about Jenna's note and asking Tori who'd actually been invited. She didn't have to wait long for a reply, because two minutes later, a new message blipped onto her screen with a flashing red exclamation point next to it.

To: NatalieNYC
From: Tori90210
Subject: Dead meat

Omigod! I am *sooooo* dead. I can't believe Jenna posted a note on the blog! That is beyond bad! I just figured you guys would check the guest list, but I should've mentioned in the Evite to keep the whole thing on the downlow. Because—this totally sucks—my parents told me I could only invite five girls from camp, so I had to pick. I haven't told the other girls about the trip yet, but now everyone's going to know! *Sob* They're going to hate me for sure. That's it, I am definitely joining the Witness Protection Program. If you never hear from me again . . . you'll know why.

Stressed out in SoCali,
Tori

Nat stared at Tori's e-mail with a sinking heart. Poor Tori. No wonder she was stressing out. If Nat were in her shoes, she wouldn't have had the first clue how to pick just five of the Lakeview girls to invite. She could tell Tori not to worry, that no one would be mad at her. All the girls loved Tori, and one little ski trip couldn't change that. Or could it? Well, even if there were hurt feelings, at least she could be there for Tori. And in the meantime, she had an awesome trip to look forward to.

▲ ▲ ▲

Brynn had never been so nervous in her entire life.

"Does Eliza Doolittle ever throw up in *My Fair Lady*?" Brynn asked her best friend, Tanya. She'd come along to the audition to offer moral support to Brynn.

"I don't think so," Tanya said. "Why?"

Brynn wiped a hand across her forehead. "'Cause I'm about to."

Tanya squeezed her shoulder. "No, you're not. The queen of the drama club would never throw up on-stage. It's totally unprofessional." She grinned. "You're going to be perfect as Eliza. They're going to love you, and you're going to get the part."

Brynn tried to smile back, but her mouth seemed frozen from fear. She knew Tanya was trying to help, but it wasn't working.

"This is the first leading role I've ever gone for at school," Brynn said.

"But what about camp?" Tanya asked. "You played leading roles for the last two years."

"That was camp," Brynn said. "This . . . is way out of my league. I don't stand a chance against Lindsay. She's a total shoo-in. She's beautiful and Miss Popular. Everyone loves her. She'll get the part just because of that."

"Eliza wasn't beautiful at the beginning of the musical, remember? She was a work in progress. Besides, you're gorgeous, dahling." Tanya laughed and waited for Brynn to crack a smile. When she didn't, Tanya gave her a gentle shake. "Get a hold of yourself! You can do this. You can recite your lines backward *and* in your sleep, you've practiced them so much."

"That's true. I think Jordan's even getting sick of hearing me practicing my fake British accent when he calls." Brynn giggled.

"I don't think Jordan could get sick of anything you do," Tanya teased. "And he better be into the British accent, because when you get the part of Eliza and he comes to opening night, he's going to hear it for two hours straight." She grinned. "You're going to invite him, aren't you?"

Brynn blushed. Even though they didn't have a lot in common at first, Jordan tried really hard to learn about what she liked and disliked. And he was doing his best to study up on theater, too. Last week when they'd talked on the phone, he'd told her that he'd rented *My*

Fair Lady so he'd know the storyline. And yesterday, Brynn had gotten a package of chocolates from him with a note that said, "Brain food for practicing the 'Wouldn't It Be Loverly' song." She thought it was the sweetest thing anyone had ever done for her.

"Sure, I'd like to invite Jordan," Brynn told Tanya, "but I have to get the part first. And that won't be easy if I faint."

"Would you stop with the theatrics already?" Tanya said, then laughed at her own joke. "You're going to be fab."

"Thanks. I hope so." Brynn sighed.

Suddenly her cell phone rang, making her jump.

When she answered, a familiar voice said, "Hello, this is the Tony Awards calling. We'd like to inform you that you've been nominated for best actress for your role in the Camp Lakeview production of *Into the Woods* that premiered last summer."

Brynn laughed. "Grace! It's so good to hear your voice!"

"Man," Grace said, "I was sure I had you going there for a minute."

"Not quite, but keep trying." Brynn smiled. Since Grace was just as into drama as she was, the two of them had bonded over the camp plays for the last couple of summers. She was sure that Grace was calling to wish her luck on her audition today. And if anyone could help Brynn get over a bad case of stage fright, Grace could. "I'm so glad you called. I really need to talk to you—"

"Me too!" Grace said. "Listen, I just wanted to let you know before you heard it from anyone else, 'cause I know that this whole ski trip thing is getting way out of control. Tori asked me not to say anything to anybody, but I don't think she meant you. Because I always tell you everything. Anyway, it turns out I was invited to go."

Brynn clutched the phone. This was what she'd been afraid of—that Grace had been invited to go and she hadn't. "Oh," she said quietly. "I mean, that's great! Really, Grace! I'm psyched for you. It's going to be so much fun."

"Yeah, but, well . . ." Grace paused. "I guess you still haven't gotten the Evite?"

"Nope." Brynn sighed. "And no e-mail from Tori, either."

"I can't believe Tori hasn't said anything to you yet," Grace said. "It sucks royally that you weren't invited."

"Yet," Brynn added, trying to be optimistic. But even as she said it, she had the sinking feeling that she hadn't been invited at all. It had been four days already since she'd found out about the Evite Tori had sent out, and she still hadn't gotten it.

"Yeah," Grace said. "Yet. It could still happen."

Brynn nodded. "But if it doesn't, I just can't believe that Tori wouldn't even e-mail the rest of us with an explanation. That makes me madder than anything else."

"Maybe she just doesn't know how to explain it without hurting someone's feelings," Grace said.

"Not saying anything hurts, too, though."

"Maybe you should call her," Grace suggested.

"That's what Alex said. That we should call her and talk to her about it." Brynn shook her head. "But I just can't deal with that until this audition is over."

"Audition!" Grace exclaimed. "What audition?"

Brynn's stomach flopped. "The *My Fair Lady* audition? I told you about it weeks ago," she said quietly.

Grace gasped. "Oh, Brynn, I'm so, so sorry. I didn't mean to forget. Really. I've just been thinking so much about the ski trip, and . . . Oh, that's no excuse. I'm being such a lousy friend. When's the audition?"

"Um, actually, it's right now," Brynn said. "That's why I thought you were calling—"

"To wish you luck!" Grace said. "Of course! You'll do great. And you know what? I just decided something. I'm not going on this ski trip unless you are. It wouldn't be fair to you. I don't want to start forgetting everyone—especially you— all because of this Evite."

Brynn gave a small smile. "Grace, it's okay. Don't worry about the audition thing. You should go on the trip, with or without me. If I were in your shoes, I'd definitely go either way."

Grace paused. "Really? I don't know . . ."

"You're going," Brynn said. "I'll figure everything out with Tori. No worries."

Just then, Mrs. Callaway, the drama club instructor, called Brynn's name, and Tanya motioned for Brynn to hang up her cell.

Brynn gasped. "Omigod, I'm up! I've got to go."

"Call me later to fill me in on how it goes," Grace said. "Bye!"

Brynn quickly hung up, but she couldn't hide her quivering lip from Tanya.

"What was that all about?" Tanya asked. "As your agent, I strongly disapprove of people causing you any sort of pain or suffering right before a big performance."

"Oh, now you're my agent, are you?" Brynn sighed. "It's this whole ski trip thing. I still can't believe I wasn't invited."

Tanya squeezed her shoulder. "Me neither. A stellar actress like you is in such high demand. Tori has no idea what a huge PR mistake she's making."

Brynn laughed. "You're crazy, you know that?"

"Only when you need a good laugh." Tanya gave her a quick hug. "Forget about the ski trip. Right now, you're a British street urchin who will soon be transformed into the fairest lady of them all."

Brynn took a deep breath, shook off her worries, and put on her best Eliza Doolittle smile. Then she stepped out from behind the curtain and onto the brightly lit stage.

"Are you ready for your audition, Brynn?" Mrs. Callaway asked, double-checking her clipboard.

"Ow, I'm bloomin' ready, all right," Brynn said in a British accent, making the casting crew seated in the audience laugh.

She would deal with Tori and the ski trip question later. For now, she was channeling her best Eliza Doolittle and hoping beyond hope that she'd get the part she was dying for.

That night as Brynn crawled into bed, she replayed the audition in her mind one more time, a huge smile growing on her face. There was no doubt about it . . . she'd nailed it. Even if she didn't get the part of Eliza, she knew she'd given it her absolute best shot. And now it was out of her hands. Just as she was fading off to sleep, her cell rang. But when she saw that it was Grace calling, she decided, for the first time ever, not to pick up. She was exhausted, and she was still hurt that Grace had forgotten about her audition, even though she knew she might be blowing the whole thing out of proportion just a little. She waited until the call went into voicemail, and then she checked her messages.

"Hey, it's me," Grace's voice said. "I was just calling to see how the audition went. I'm sure you blew everyone away! Anyways, I'm sorry—again—for forgetting about it before. That was a total brain fart. Call me when you get a sec. I want to hear your British accent!"

Brynn listened to the message twice, and then felt a sudden pang of guilt. Wasn't she being pretty tough on Grace? She wasn't mad at Grace, but about this whole ski trip in general. The truth was, she didn't understand why Grace had been invited and she hadn't. And that was what hurt more than anything.

chapter

THREE

Tori nearly dropped her nail polish all over her math homework when her cell rang.

"Can you see who it is?" she asked Michael, who had come over to help her study for the algebra test she had tomorrow.

Michael checked the caller ID. "It's Alyssa."

"Oh!" Tori smiled in relief and grabbed the phone. Since she'd sent out the Evite last Saturday, Brynn, Alex, Chelsea, and Priya had all tried calling her, but Tori had let her voicemail pick up every time. Ever since Nat had e-mailed her to tell her about the blog entry Jenna'd posted spilling the beans to *everyone* about the trip, Tori'd been keeping a very low profile. She wanted to pretend that everything was okay, at least for a little while longer. She knew Jenna, Grace, and Sarah were definitely coming on the ski trip, though, which made her feel better. Nat and Alyssa were still working out their tickets, but she hoped that Alyssa was calling her with good news. And sure enough, when Tori picked up, Alyssa told her she'd booked her flight.

"But," Alyssa added after Tori's initial excitement died down, "I actually called to talk to you about something else."

"Okay," Tori said, even though her heart had started racing. She had a feeling she knew what was coming.

"Have you talked to the other girls from camp?" Alyssa asked. "I mean, I know what the deal is with your parents and the ski trip, but not everybody else does. And it's not fair to just keep them in the dark about it. We're all going to see each other at the camp reunion, and it'll be super-awkward if nobody ever talks about it."

"I know." Tori sighed. "But I don't have a clue how to explain who I picked to come on the trip."

"That's a tough one," Alyssa said. "I mean, we all know why Chelsea didn't make the cut." She laughed.

"That's not very nice, Lyss," Tori said, then paused. "True, but not very nice."

"Okay, okay," Alyssa said. "I take it back . . . sort of. But I think you just have to be honest with everybody. You don't have to give specifics about why you picked who you did, or even *who* you picked, but you still owe the rest of your friends an explanation, don't you think?"

"I know," Tori said. "I should've done it way before this, when I first saw Jenna's blog entry. I'll do it tonight."

"And I'll e-mail you my flight itinerary as soon as I have it," Alyssa said. "But I'm just warning you. I'm a much better painter than I am a skier."

"After a weekend with me, you'll be flying down those black diamonds," Tori said. "Of course, it may be on your butt, but you'll be flying."

Alyssa laughed. "I've gotta go. Nat and I are trying to get on the same flight as Jenna, so I've got to give her a call before I go over my cell minutes."

"Okay," Tori said. "I'm really glad you're coming on the trip."

After Tori hung up, Michael glanced up from his algebra book.

"So?" he said. "Everything okay?"

"I'm not really sure," Tori said. "Alyssa was fine, but she's right. I have to stop being such a chicken and get back to the girls about this trip." She gave Michael an apologetic smile. "Can we take a ten-minute break from studying so I can write some e-mails?"

"No problem," Michael said, grabbing the remote for Tori's TV from her nightstand. "Just let me know when you're ready to get back into X plus Y equals Z."

Tori groaned. "I may never be ready. Did you forget how much I hate math?"

"Nope," Michael said. "But that's why I'm here . . . to make sure you stick with it."

"Yeah. How lucky am I to have you?" Tori said teasingly.

She took a deep breath, and then logged onto her computer to post the blog message she'd been dreading for so long. She'd send out a blanket apology on the camp blog to all the girls from 4A and 4C who hadn't been invited, and hopefully that would at least be a start in the right direction. But before she clicked on the blog site she checked her e-mail, then immediately wished she hadn't. There were three e-mails waiting for her from Chelsea, Brynn, and Alex. She cringed as she read Chelsea's:

To: Tori90210
From: Chelsea1
Subject: How to Lose Friends and Disappoint People

Tori,
I can't believe you'd exclude so many of us from your posh ski weekend and not even have the guts to tell us to our faces. I checked with Karen, Valerie, and Priya, and none of us got the Evite. But the worst part is, you didn't even explain why. Nice show of friendship. Well, don't worry. Even if you did invite me and Karen now, there's no way we would go as your "second choices." Thanks for not thinking of us. Have a great trip.
Chelsea

Tears welled up in Tori's eyes as she reread the e-mail three more times. Then she finally got up the courage to read Alex and Brynn's e-mails, too, and was at least a little relieved to see that theirs weren't nearly as awful.

I'm pretty sure I'm not invited on your ski trip, Brynn's e-mail said, *but I wanted to double-check in case, you know, there was mistake or something. It'd be great to hear from you either way, Tori. I'd just like to know for sure.*

Alex's e-mail wasn't as mean as Chelsea's either, but she said how disappointed she was that Tori hadn't even sent out an explanation about the trip.

Tori closed her e-mail and let her head sink to her desktop.

"Hey," Michael said, clicking off the TV, "what's the damage? It can't be that bad, can it?"

"Yes," Tori murmured, "it can. Chelsea's fuming, and Brynn and Alex are hurt, too. This is way worse than I expected."

"What are you going to do?" Michael asked.

Tori sighed. "I can't just post a note on the blog. That's how this whole thing got messed up in the first place. I'll have to e-mail each of the girls to explain everything. Right now."

Michael nodded. "That makes sense. But I guess this means no more studying tonight."

"Oh, I'll be studying," Tori said. "But it won't be until after I've done this. And believe me, even algebra is sounding better to me right now than sending these e-mails."

"I hear you," Michael said, gathering his stuff together. "Well, call me if you need help with equations later. Or if you just need to talk."

Tori gave his hand a squeeze. "Thanks."

Once he'd left, Tori turned back to her e-mail. First she knocked out one to Brynn, explaining everything about her parents' stupid five-person rule, and apologizing for not being able to invite everyone. She read the e-mail half a dozen times and then finally clicked Send. Well, that one wasn't so awful. She actually felt a little better now that she'd finally done it. And she'd managed to avoid mentioning the names of the five girls she had invited, which was a lot easier than having to get into specifics. She'd e-mail Alex, Valerie, and Priya next, and then keep going until she'd e-mailed all the girls. If she wanted to go back to camp next summer with all of her friendships intact, this was her only chance.

▲ ▲ ▲

Sarah slam-dunked the basketball through the hoop just as the final buzzer rang, and landed on her feet to the cheers of the other girls on her team.

"Score one more for the winning team!" Abby shouted, high-fiving her. "That was an awesome shot."

"Thanks," Sarah said, grinning as they put the balls back into the phys ed storage room.

"I still wish they'd let us play some kind of sport outside, though," Abby said, crinkling her nose. "I hate the musty way the school gym smells in winter."

"I hear that." Sarah nodded. "They should offer sledding in phys ed. That's aerobic."

"Or cross-country skiing." Abby grinned. "That would be really cool."

Sarah's insides froze. Had Abby mentioned skiing on purpose to see if she'd get a reaction out of Sarah? Had she found out about Sarah buying the ticket to Tahoe? Sarah couldn't imagine how she would've found out, unless . . . maybe Tori had told her. Or Nat. Sarah had seen the blog Jenna'd posted about the trip, but she knew that Abby wasn't into checking the camp blog that often. "I can't sit still for that long," Abby'd once explained when they were talking about the Internet. "At least if I'm on the phone, I can walk around kicking a soccer ball."

She shook off her uneasiness. This was ridiculous. If she'd only told Abby she'd been invited on the trip from the beginning, she wouldn't be a complete paranoid freak right now. But telling her about it now—almost a week after the fact—seemed, well, pretty much impossible.

"Hey!" Abby waved a hand in front of Sarah's face. "Zombie-girl, snap out of it! Do I have a mongo-zit on my chin or something?"

Sarah blinked, coming back to reality. "No. Why?"

Abby leaned forward and slugged her playfully on the arm. "Because you were staring at me like I'd just grown two wings and a pair of fangs. What's up?"

Sarah shrugged, dunking the last of the basket-balls into the ball bag. "Nothing. I was just wondering when our camp reunion is going to be. It'll be great to see David again."

"I should've known that look on your face was boy-related." Abby grinned. "I'm sure you'll get to see your boy before the winter thaw. I don't know anything about the reunion, but I finally got around to checking the camp blog during study hall this morning and there was a note from Jenna about some ski trip Tori's planning to Tahoe. Did you see that?"

Sarah heart shuddered. So Abby had seen the blog after all. Great . . . now what was she supposed to say? "Um," she stalled, thinking fast. "Yeah, I saw it. But at first I couldn't figure out what Jenna was talking about, so I didn't think it was a big deal. I never got an Evite from Tori." She couldn't believe she'd just lied like that to Abby. What was her problem?

"Me neither," said Abby, still not showing any signs of anger. "And then, after I read Jenna's post, I logged onto my e-mail for the first time this month and there was this totally strange note from Tori. She sent it last night, and it went on and on about how she was really sorry that not everyone could come to Tahoe. But she never said who she ended up inviting. How ridiculous is that? Did you get an e-mail from her, too?"

"Uh huh." Sarah nodded. "Mine said the same thing." She was lying right and left and all over the place now. "I guess that means neither one of us was invited."

Abby shrugged. "Well, that's good. At least we're outcasts together, right?" She giggled. "I don't get what all the drama's about, anyway. I don't care that she didn't invite me to go."

"You don't?" Sarah asked, surprised.

"Nah. My parents could never afford to send me, not with my brother and sister both in college this year. Besides, we'll get to see everyone at the reunion, no biggie."

"Yeah, I guess." Sarah took a deep breath. Now was her chance to tell Abby the truth. If Abby really didn't care about the trip, would she care that Sarah was going without her? Probably not. But then again, what if she did? Even though lying to her friend about the trip didn't feel right, wasn't it better to protect Abby from being hurt? "I wouldn't have been able to go skiing in Tahoe, either," Sarah said. "My parents are taking me out to visit my grandma in Maine that weekend."

"They are?" Abby asked, surprise in her voice. "You never said anything about it before."

"Yeah, I know," Sarah bumbled. "It just came up at the last minute. We're going to drive up." This was turning into lie after lie, and now she couldn't stop herself. "Skiing would have been better than visiting my grandma, trust me," she said, laughing nervously. "She's kind of a grump." Well, that part was true, at least.

"Hey," Abby nudged Sarah and pointed out the gym window, where snow was starting to fall fast. "If this snow keeps up and they don't cancel school, we may have to try skiing home. So who needs Tahoe?"

Sarah smiled. "You forget, we don't have skis."

Abby slapped her forehead melodramatically. "Oh, right. So, whose mom do we call to pick us up from school? Yours or mine?"

Sarah panicked. She'd forgotten all about their snow rule. Usually, her mom and Abby's took turns picking them up in bad weather. But today, her mom had promised to take her shopping for a new ski jacket after school. And if Abby came along, then Sarah'd have to confess the whole awful truth. She just couldn't do it. Not today, not any day.

"Actually," she said, feeling shame coloring her face, "my mom's already picking me up, but she has to run some errands for her work right afterward. I promised I'd help her, but I'll spare you the torture. And the thing is, she's not going to have time to drop you off before the errands."

"Oh." Abby's face fell ever so slightly, but she quickly pulled on a nonchalant expression. "No problem. I'll give my mom a call. She's been complaining lately about how we never get any mother-daughter bonding time together anymore. I guess a car ride alone with her might keep her happy for a while."

Sarah laughed. This was what she loved about Abby—her laid back, go-with-the-flow style.

The bell rang, signaling that the girls had five minutes to get to their next class.

"I better get a move on," Sarah said. "I still have to change out of my gym clothes."

"I'm going to rinse off real quick," Abby said, heading for the showers. "I'll see you later. And try to stop daydreaming about David. Too much thinking about guys kills brain cells, you know."

Sarah laughed, but as she turned to head to her locker, the smile faded from her face. She was sinking deeper into a web of lies with Abby, and as much as she loved their new friendship, she had no idea how to dig her way out of this one.

chapter

FOUR

Nat had never seen so many clothes in her entire life, and for a minute she felt like she'd died and gone to shopper's heaven. The racks of ski pants, jackets, hats, and gloves, stretched out for what seemed like miles in all directions. If she couldn't find a fab ski outfit in this place, it would be a sin against all good fashion sense.

"I think we've rendered Nat speechless," Jenna teased, elbowing Alyssa and Grace.

"Nah." Hannah grinned at Nat. "She's just a newbie to Jersey outlet shopping."

Jenna had called Nat yesterday to invite her and Hannah (Nat's NY BFF) out to New Jersey for a Saturday shopping spree at the massive Sports Authority Outlet in the New Jersey Commons, and Nat suddenly felt like a whole new wonderful world of discount designer clothing had been opened up to her.

She walked from rack to rack, running her hands through the rainbow of colored fabrics. Soon, her arms were spilling over with mounds of jackets and pants to try on.

"Alyssa!" she cried, trying in vain to see over her armful. "Do you know where the dressing room is?"

Somewhere to her right, she heard Alyssa and Grace break into giggling fits. Alyssa grabbed some of the clothes off Nat's pile, which she could do easily, since she'd only picked one funky metallic-blue snowsuit to try on.

"Follow me," Alyssa said. "And by the way, have you ever thought about joining shopaholics anonymous?"

"Hey," Nat said. "I haven't bought anything yet. I'm just trying on."

"Sure, Nat," Hannah teased, following her into the dressing room with Grace and Jenna. "That's what you said last time you spent three months' allowance on clothes."

"Critics," Nat mumbled before closing her dressing room door. Ten minutes and twenty outfits later, she found the perfect fit—a cotton-candy-pink jacket with sleek charcoal pants to match.

"Snow bunny central," Hannah said, nodding in approval.

"What about me?" Jenna said, stepping out of her dressing room. She had on a huge jester-style hat with points that hung all the way down to her waist, a pair of pants that were three sizes too big and on backward, and a kid-size jacket adorned with SpongeBob SquarePants decals.

Nat, Alyssa, and Grace all cracked up.

"You look fantastic," Alyssa said. "If you're going for a demented clown look."

"All right, all right," Jenna joked. "I'll lose SpongeBob, but I'm keeping the hat. You guys are going to be eating my powder!"

Suddenly Nat's cell phone rang and she nearly dropped the pair of ski gloves she was holding. Her stomach knotted before she even looked at the caller ID. She had a feeling she knew who was calling her, and as soon as she saw Simon's name pop up, she sent him straight into voicemail.

"It's Simon," Nat said to the girls. "I'll call him back later."

"Um, hello?" Hannah said. "Since when do you screen Simon's calls? Normally you dive for the phone when it's him."

"Yeah," Jenna said. "And Adam told me that Simon told *him* that you've been acting a little weird lately."

"Omigod . . . Simon said that?" Nat's heart hammered. "I didn't think he noticed."

"He's not that oblivious," Alyssa said. "So spill it. What's the prob?"

"I don't know." Nat stared at the gloves in her hands, not even feeling the slightest desire to try them on anymore, which meant she was in really bad shape. "When we talk on the phone lately, there are these long periods of silence, where I can't think of a single thing to say."

"No way," Grace said. "You're exaggerating."

Nat shot her a look. "I counted an entire minute of absolute silence in our last conversation."

"Okay," Alyssa said. "So you're not exaggerating."

Nat sighed, nodding. "He wanted to come into

the city this weekend to stay with Rick, but I told him I was busy with you guys. Normally, I would have changed all my plans to spend time with him. I don't know what's wrong with me."

"What about trying to date other guys?" Alyssa asked, gathering up her clothes to take them to the cash register. "You and Simon never set rules about dating other people."

"But I'd feel horrible knowing that Simon was waiting around for me to call him while I was on a date with some other guy."

"Maybe he wouldn't be," Hannah said. "Maybe he feels the same way, too. You could talk to him about it and find out."

"Right," Nat said. "I don't even have the guts to talk to half our friends about the ski trip. I am obviously challenged in the art of awkward conversations."

"Join the club," Jenna said. "We're all having trouble there. It's the guilt factor."

"I felt bad not telling Brynn about this shopping spree," Grace said.

"We still have the reunion to straighten everything out with the girls," Nat said. "But that still leaves Simon."

Hannah gave Nat's hand a squeeze. "You'll figure everything out. But right now we need to focus on the perfect accessories for your jacket. Do you want to look totally glam for this ski trip or not?"

Nat grinned. "Totally glam. And I think this ivory hat has my name on it." She grabbed it off the top of her pile. "I'll model, you guys critique. Tahoe skiing, here we come!"

▲ ▲ ▲

Brynn clutched her bag tighter and tighter, her heart hammering. She was dying to check the cast list to find out if she'd gotten the part of Eliza in *My Fair Lady*, but her rubber-chicken legs flat out refused to walk the few feet to the white sheet of paper hanging on the auditorium door. But when she saw Tanya heading toward her, a determined look on her face, she knew there was no getting out of it.

"Did you look? Did you look?" Tanya blurted out.

Brynn had to smile at her friend. "Not yet," she admitted, then gave a weak laugh when Tanya gaped at her. "I needed to prepare myself first."

"For what?" Tanya said, rolling her eyes. "A tragedy? Are you so sure it's going to be bad news?"

Brynn took a deep breath. "I . . . I'm afraid it is."

Tanya grabbed Brynn's hand and playfully pulled her toward the cast list. "Come on," Tanya said. "If you don't look, I will. The suspense is killing me."

Together, they took a few steps closer to the door until Brynn could see the names on the list clearly. She found Lindsay's first, and as soon as she saw it, her mouth dropped open.

"Lindsay got the part of Professor Higgins's mother," Brynn said between quiet giggles. "She's only got about three lines in the whole play."

Tanya laughed. "I knew it. You can't be cheerleading captain, resident beauty queen, and honors student without being challenged in some area. I guess drama isn't her thing. But it sure is yours." With that, she pointed to Brynn's name, written next to the words: *Eliza Doolittle*.

Brynn did a celebratory dance and hugged Tanya. "I can't believe I got the part!" She quickly skimmed the rest of the flyer, making a mental note of rehearsal dates, which—yikes!—started Tuesday, January 23. That was tomorrow!

"I told you there was nothing to worry about," Tanya said. "Come on, let's celebrate. We can grab decaf mochas from the Au Lait Café on our way home. My treat."

"Sounds great," Brynn said, feeling her face glowing warm with happiness. "But wait, I should call Jordan first. And I have to e-mail the girls from camp to let them know, too." As soon as the words left her mouth, some of the initial thrill she'd felt at getting the part faded.

"Wait a minute," Tanya said, frowning. "You're not talking about the girls who are going on the ski trip without you?"

"No, I'm definitely going to tell Alex, Priya, and the other girls who aren't going to Tahoe," Brynn said as they walked to the café. "But I haven't decided whether or not to tell the other girls who are going."

"I still can't believe they're excluding you like that."

"It's not their faults," Brynn said, trying halfheartedly to defend her friends. "Tori was the one who picked who to invite, and she feels horrible about it. And I don't blame the other girls for going. It sounds like an awesome trip."

"But why should you include them in your life when they're not including you in theirs?" Tanya asked. "You're being way too understanding if you ask me. I'd be really mad."

"I'm mad that we can't *all* go," Brynn said. "And I'm mad that the whole trip has made things tense between all of us. And Grace . . ." She sighed. "She's called and e-mailed me three times in the last week, but I haven't returned any of her calls. I keep thinking that if I'd been invited to Tahoe and Grace hadn't, I wouldn't have gone. And even though it's completely warped, that makes me peeved at Grace. It's like, I want to tell her about the play, but at the same time . . . I kind of don't. Am I just being a big baby about the whole thing?"

"I don't think so, and I don't think you're overreacting, either," Tanya said.

Brynn stopped walking and stared at the ground, debating. Then she pulled out her cell phone. "No, you know what? This is stupid. The ski trip shouldn't come between me and Grace. Nothing should. I'm going to call her right now."

Tanya nodded while Brynn dialed. The line rang a couple of times, and then finally, Grace picked up.

"Grace?" Brynn said, her heart speeding up. "Um, it's Brynn."

"Hi!" Grace said. "Did you get all my messages?"

"Yeah, um, that's why I'm calling," Brynn said,

swallowing down the awkward feeling in her chest. "I just wanted to tell you, I—"

"Hey, Brynn?" Grace interrupted. "I really want to hear this, but I'm on the other line with Tori giving her my flight info for the ski trip. Can I call you right back?"

Brynn's smile dropped off her face. "That's okay," she said quietly. "It wasn't important. Don't worry about calling me back."

"But I want to," Grace said, sounding worried. "I just have to finish up with Tori."

"Just forget I called," Brynn said, trying to sound nonchalant. "It's no biggie. Really. Tell Tori I said hi. Bye." She clicked her phone shut.

"You okay?" Tanya asked, seeing the waterworks building up that Brynn was trying so hard to hide.

"Yeah," Brynn whispered. "I guess I shouldn't have called her after all."

"Do you want to talk about it?" Tanya asked.

Brynn shook her head. "Not really."

Tanya nodded. "Okay. Then I have another idea. Why don't you call Jordan? You'll feel way better after you invite him to the play. Besides, it's about time I get to meet this guy."

Brynn took a deep breath. "I don't know. What if he blows me off, too? I can't handle rejection twice in one day."

"Are you kidding?" Tanya said. "Any guy who would sit through the entire movie of *My Fair Lady* has to be crazy about you. There's no way he'll say no."

"I hope you're right," Brynn said. She dialed Jordan's number with trembling fingers, and when he answered, she felt a mixture of nervousness and excitement.

"Did you get the part?" he asked right away.

Brynn beamed, so glad he'd remembered. "Yeah, I did. And . . . you should totally come see the play opening night, it's in about three weeks, on February 10." The words rushed out of her because she figured if she didn't say them all in one breath, she'd panic and freeze up. The next few seconds seemed to take whole centuries to pass, but then Jordan practically shouted into the phone.

"That's awesome, Brynn! I knew you'd get the part. And I'll definitely come. There's no way I could pass up a chance to see you as a leading lady."

Brynn blushed and gave Tanya the thumbs-up sign to show her that Jordan had said yes. "Great!" Tanya mouthed.

Brynn talked with Jordan for a few more minutes, feeling happier than she had for most of the day. She almost forgot all about her awful conversation with Grace, and by the time she hung up with Jordan, she was in a good mood again.

As she sat down at the coffee shop with Tanya, she thought about how lucky she was. She'd gotten her first role as the leading lady in a school play, and her boyfriend and her best friend would both be there to cheer for her on opening night.

When she got home, she e-mailed Alex and

invited her to come to the play, too, and Alex agreed in a heartbeat. But even though she was on cloud nine, Brynn still felt a hole in her heart where she was missing the rest of her camp friends and wishing things could go back to the way they used to be.

chapter FIVE

Tori ran the bar of warm wax slowly over her skis, careful not to let any drip on her bedroom carpet. She knew it was a little early to be getting everything ready for Tahoe, but she wanted to make sure the whole weekend was perfect. She'd already taken her ski boots into the sports shop for tightening, and her mom had agreed to buy her some new lavender ski pants to go with her ivory coat. Now all she had left to do was wax her skis and, when the time came, pack her clothes. Just as she was finishing up, the IM icon on her computer started flashing.

<Aries8>: Tori! Are u there? We have a serious problem. Did you get the invite to the reunion?
<Tori90210>: Hi, Jenna. No, no invite, but I haven't checked the mail today. What's wrong?
<Aries8>: Well, brace yourself . . . the reunion's over Presidents' Day weekend. The same weekend as Tahoe. What are we going to do?

Tori's heart dropped to her toes, through the floor, and into the basement. Her hands were trembling so badly that she could barely keep typing. This couldn't be happening. It just couldn't.

<Tori90210>: I can talk to my parents. Maybe we can plan the ski trip for the weekend after the reunion instead.
<Aries8>: That would be great, but here's the thing. I already checked with Nat and Alyssa, and all our tickets are nonrefundable.

Tori gripped the edge of her desk. Oh, no. This was all her fault. She was the one who'd told everyone to book their tickets through CheapFlightz because of the great rates. And now she felt sick to her stomach about the whole thing.

<Tori90210>: OMG. I can't believe this is happening.
<Aries8>: Me neither. I've never missed a reunion for as long as I've been a camper at Lakeview.
<Tori90210>: U don't have to come skiing if you'd rather go to the reunion. I'd completely understand.
<Aries8>: I already tried to convince my parents to let me cancel the ticket to Tahoe. My dad looked like he was about ready to pop a blood vessel or something, so I dropped it. It's a lost cause.
<Tori90210>: I'm so sorry. Maybe we can set up a conference call tonight with everyone coming on the ski trip to see if there's anything we can do.
<Aries8>: K
<Tori90210>: Talk 2 u tonight.

Tori logged off and walked out to the mailbox. There it was, right on top of the pile of today's mail. She opened the envelope with the Camp Lakeview letterhead and read:

Greetings, Lakeview Campers! It's that time of year again! Forget the winter blues at the annual camp reunion. We hope to see all of you there!

Where: Wollman Skating Rink in Central Park, New York City
When: Saturday, February 17
Why: To make even more great Lakeview memories!
Time: 4:00 P.M.–10:00 P.M.

Dear Lakeview Alumni,

Join us to reunite with old friends and meet brand new ones at the annual camp reunion. This year, we'll make the best of Manhattan's winter wonderland by ice-skating in Central Park. The winter Olympics will be put to shame by our freestyle Ice Capades competition. (You might want to bring a helmet for this one. Nah, just kidding.)

Broom hockey, an obstacle course, and ice disco are just a few of the fun activities we have planned for you. Skate till you drop, and then reenergize with us at the Jekyll & Hyde Club for a fun-filled dinner worthy of all you mad scientists out there. You can feast on a Frankenburger while you're enjoying the dinner show, and finish up a fantastic night with your Lakeview friends. We look forward to seeing you all!

    Please RSVP by February 5.
    Yours,
    Dr. Steve

Tori stared at the invitation for a long time before slowly heading inside. She barely made it to her room before the tears started falling, and they kept coming until her mom called her to dinner. She washed her face with cold water in the hopes of hiding some of the puffiness around her eyes, then finally gave up and dragged herself to the table. But nothing on her plate looked even remotely appetizing. All she could think about was how she'd let everyone down.

"Earth to Tori," her dad finally said. "You haven't been this quiet since before you were born." He laughed at his own joke, but Tori didn't even have the energy to roll her eyes at his horrible sense of humor. "Don't you want to nag us about all the things we need to do to get ready for your big ski trip?"

"Yeah," her mom added. "For the last week it's been all you've talked about. I was expecting you to give us more marching orders tonight. What's wrong, hon?"

Fresh tears sprang up in Tori's eyes. "It's about the ski trip," she started, her voice cracking. "I just found out it's the same weekend as our camp reunion."

"Oh, sweetie, that's too bad," her mom said, giving Tori's hand a squeeze. "But I'm sure everyone will understand why you and the other girls can't make it."

"No, Mom," Tori said. "I don't think they will. Half of the girls aren't even speaking to me since I couldn't invite them to Tahoe, and now Nat, Alyssa, Jenna, Sarah, and Grace are all going to be upset, too."

Tori pushed her food around on her plate, and suddenly, an idea came to her. "You guys agreed to pay for lift tickets, food, and ski rentals for Tahoe. But what if we use the money to pay for the girls' plane tickets out here instead? That way they can cancel their tickets without having to pay for them, and then we can all go to the reunion." Tori paused to let the idea sink in with her dad. It was a long shot, but she had to at least try.

Her mom and dad exchanged one of those parenting "looks" Tori'd always hated. And right then and there, she knew there was no hope.

"We're sorry this is turning out to be so hard for you, hon," her mom said. "But paying for your friends' plane tickets wasn't part of our original plan. And canceling the tickets on such short notice is going to cost more than rentals and lift tickets would." Her mom gave her a sympathetic smile. "You and the girls are going to have to figure out a way to make this work on your own."

Tori opened her mouth to argue, but then

thought better of it. What was the point? She knew once her parents made up their minds, there was no changing them.

"Can I please be excused?" Tori said. "I'm not hungry, and I want to call the girls to talk to them about this."

Her dad nodded. "Sure, honey. We'll stick your plate in the fridge in case you get hungry later and want to heat it up." He kissed her on the forehead. "And don't worry. Your friends will be all right, and so will you."

Tori climbed the stairs to her bedroom with the feeling that she was climbing to a torture chamber. Once she'd changed into her yoga pants and curled up on her bed, hugging her pillow for support, she conference-called Alyssa, Jenna, Nat, Sarah, and Grace. When all of them were on the line, she took a deep breath and began.

"I'm guessing you guys already know why I called," she said.

"Yeah," Alyssa said. "We all got the invites to the reunion today, too."

"I'm so, so sorry," Tori whispered, barely able to get out the words for fear of crying again.

"Hey, no apologies," Sarah said. "None of us had any way of knowing that the reunion would be on the same weekend."

"I know," Tori said, "but I feel awful that you guys are going to miss out on seeing everyone else. And I'm going to miss my first reunion ever!"

"That *is* a bummer," Jenna said. "I forgot this was your first year at camp. But hey, there's always next year, right?"

Tori sniffled. "Listen, are you guys okay? I mean, *really* okay with this? Because if you'd rather go to the reunion and you want to cancel, I won't be mad. Really."

"No way!" Nat exclaimed. "We'd never back out on you. Besides, the ski trip is still going to be so much fun."

"That's right," Grace jumped in. "I've been to the reunion before, but I've never, ever been skiing. I'd be crazy to miss out on this trip."

Alyssa chimed in with, "And we can always plan a mini camp reunion later in the year for all the girls from 4A and 4C, right?"

A half-smile spread on Tori's face. "Thanks for being so understanding, guys. I'm just really sorry that I put you in this position."

"Okay, girlfriend," Nat said. "That's enough stressing for one night. Go get some beauty rest. 'Cause you won't be getting much sleep on the ski trip. We have way too much gossiping and too many spa treatments to catch up on."

Tori laughed. "You guys are the greatest. Talk to you later."

After she hung up, she was actually feeling a little bit better . . . until she checked her e-mail. And there it was, a two-sentence note from Chelsea that said what Tori knew everyone was thinking, even if they weren't saying it.

To: Tori90210
From: Chelsea1
Subject: Camp reunion

Good job ruining the reunion for everyone. Now no one can enjoy it, thanks to you.

Tears welled up in Tori's eyes all over again. Even though no one else but Chelsea had the guts to say it, Tori knew it was true. No matter how she looked at it, the camp reunion, and maybe the ski trip, too, was ruined, and it was all her fault.

⛺ ⛺ ⛺

<SarahSports>: Hey, fellow Tahoe-goers. How are you feeling today? I couldn't sleep after we talked to Tori last night.

<Grrrrace>: I couldn't sleep last night, either. I kept thinking about Brynn. I know she's mad at me and I was really hoping I'd have a chance to make things up to her at the reunion. But now who knows when I'll see her next?

<SarahSports>: Ditto that with Abby. You guys don't know this, but I did something horrible to her. If she finds out, we might not be friends anymore.

<Alyssa11>: What?!? You guys are so close . . . nothing could ever change that.

<Aries8>: Let us know if u want to talk about it later, k? We're here.

<SarahSports>: K.

<Alyssa11>: Listen, I know none of us wants to upset Tori, so let's make sure we have our happy faces on for the ski trip.

<NatalieNYC>: yeah, we're still going to have a great time in tahoe, right?

<Aries8>: Right!

Sarah clicked off her instant messenger and sighed. She wished she could tell the other girls how she'd lied to Abby, but she couldn't even type it. It made her feel sick to her stomach just thinking about it. She needed a distraction in the worst way, so she took out her brand-new sunshine yellow ski jacket from the closet again. Her mom had finally agreed to let her buy it last week after Sarah promised to take on a few extra babysitting jobs to help pay for it. It was bright and fun and perfect for West Coast skiing, she hoped. But for the first time since she'd bought it, looking at it didn't give her a thrill of excitement. Now, it just reminded her that while she'd be wearing it in Tahoe, the rest of her friends, including Abby, would be ice-skating in New York at the reunion. She hated that she wasn't as excited about Tahoe as she had been, and her poor jacket didn't seem as perfect as it had before, even with the price tag still on it.

It was cold enough to wear her new jacket to school, but she couldn't risk it—not with Abby. Abby would ask her all about it, and then what would Sarah say? She hadn't talked to Abby since the reunion invitation had come, but she'd see her at school tomorrow, and then she'd have to lie some more about her grandma.

Sarah picked up the jacket from her bed and

headed to the closet to hang it up. When she turned around, Abby was standing in her bedroom doorway. Sarah had no idea how long Abby had been standing there, or whether she had seen the jacket.

"Hi!" Sarah said, a little too enthusiastically. "What are you doing here?" she asked, sitting down on her bed as nonchalantly as she could.

Abby's eyes stayed on the closed closet door. "I came over to talk to you about the reunion. I just got the invite yesterday. I can't believe it's over Presidents' Day weekend. That's when you're going to see your grandma, right?"

Sarah swallowed. Here came all the lies. "Yeah," she said. "It totally sucks. I spent all last night trying to convince my parents to let me go the reunion instead, but they're not budging."

"Uh huh," Abby said, but her expression was rapidly changing from calm to furious. "Why don't you just tell me what's really going on?"

"What do you mean?" Sarah asked, starting to feel panicky.

"I mean you can quit the innocent act," Abby said fiercely. "I couldn't get ahold of you this morning, so I e-mailed Priya to talk to her about it, and she told me that she didn't know anything about your grandma, but she did know that you were going on the ski trip to Tahoe with Tori. At first I didn't believe her, but now that I've seen your new ski jacket, I know it's true." Abby's voice rose into a yell. "You've been lying to me all this time, haven't you?"

Sarah bit her lip, trying to fight back the tears,

but they spilled over onto her cheeks. "I'm so sorry, Abby. I didn't mean to lie, really I didn't. The whole thing just got so out of control, and I didn't want to hurt your feelings, and—"

"Hurt my feelings?" Abby shouted, cutting her off. "You did that when you started lying to me. I thought we were great friends, but I was so wrong. A friend would never do something like this."

"Abby, please," Sarah sobbed.

"No." Abby turned toward the door. "Saying you're sorry won't work. I can't trust you anymore." Now she looked like she was going to start crying, too. "Have fun on the ski trip. And don't bother calling me when you get back."

As soon as the door slammed, Sarah fell on her bed and began sobbing. She cried until there weren't any tears left. Then, just when she was feeling completely drained, inspiration dawned on her. Maybe there was a way to fix things with Abby before she lost her best friend forever. A half an hour later, Sarah'd gotten her mom to agree with her idea, and she was anxiously dialing Tori's cell.

"I need to talk to you about the ski trip," Sarah told Tori as soon as she picked up.

"You're not coming?" Tori asked quietly.

Sarah paused, and then sighed. "I really hate this, but yeah . . . I don't think I am. I talked to my mom, and we worked out an agreement. I'm going to take on some more babysitting jobs and pay her back for the ticket so that I can cancel it. This ski trip is ruining my whole friendship with Abby, and I have to make things right with her."

Sarah was met with silence on the other end of the line. "Tori? Are you there? Are you okay?"

It took a minute before Tori spoke again and when she did, it was through sniffles. "You're right. You should do whatever you have to do to work it out with Abby, but I wish you were coming skiing with us, too."

"Me too," Sarah said. "But this feels like the right thing to do."

Tori sighed. "You're right. I'm sure Abby will come around when you tell her what you decided."

"I hope so," Sarah said.

"I made it hard on everyone when I planned this trip," Tori said. "And I was just trying to do something nice."

"We know you were," Sarah said. "This is just how everything worked out. And you guys are still going to have a great time, you know. If Abby doesn't start speaking to me again, I'm going to wish I was out there with you guys instead."

"She won't be mad at you anymore when she finds out that you canceled your trip."

"I hope not," Sarah said. "The reunion won't be the same without all of us together, though, even if Abby is speaking to me again."

"I know," Tori said. "That's how I feel about the ski trip, too."

"I'm sorry for backing out on you at the last minute," Sarah said. "Are you sure you're not mad?"

"How can I be?" Tori said. "I'm just wishing you

could be in two places at once, that's all." She gave a small laugh.

Sarah smiled. "You and me both. Take lots of pictures for me, okay?"

"Definitely," Tori said. "And you take lots at the reunion, too. I want details of the whole weekend."

"We can swap albums afterward," Sarah said. "I'll miss you, though."

"You too," Tori said. "Now go call Abby."

"Thanks, Tori," Sarah said, "for being such a good friend and for being so understanding."

As soon as Sarah hung up the phone, she dialed Abby's number to tell her the good news, but Abby wouldn't pick up. Even when Sarah tried her a second time.

"Hey, Abby, I just wanted you to know that I've decided to go to the reunion instead of Tahoe. Isn't that great? Call me back." As Sarah snapped her phone closed, she felt a sneaking sense that Abby wouldn't call her right back. Which was okay with Sarah. Abby might not forgive Sarah right away, but Sarah would keep trying to make up with her until she did.

**To: BrynnWins; SoccerLover; Pree; Chelsea1;
SleepyKaren; Valfrog
From: NatalieNYC
Subject: Reunion weekend**

hi alex, brynn, chelsea, val, karen, and priya,

i hate to write this in an e-mail, but i tried calling all of you and can't get through. i'm really, really sorry about this, but you guys can't stay over at my place on the weekend of the reunion. my ticket to tahoe is nonrefundable, and mom won't let me cancel it. i tried to convince her to let you stay over at the apartment anyway, but she's got a busy work schedule and feels uncomfortable leaving everyone alone without me. i feel really awful about this whole thing, because i know i made you all a promise. but there's nothing I can do about it. i hope you won't be too angry with me. i know the reunion's less than two weeks away, but i'm sure you'll still be able to find a hotel in the city for that weekend. please, please, PLEASE write back or call me asap so that we can talk. i miss all of you, and i don't

want this to mess up our friendships.
    sincerely sorry in manhattan,
    nat

For Nat, this was the day that would never end. She'd already tried calling all the girls from camp who she'd said could sleep over for the reunion weekend, but she couldn't get through to anyone, and she had the sneaking suspicion that they were ignoring her. She'd sent out an e-mail, too, as a last resort, but she'd checked her account about a thousand times today, and no one had written back. It was becoming painfully clear: Everyone that wasn't going on the ski trip was mad at Nat for retracting her reunion invite. And Nat had no idea what she could say or do to make it better.

She logged onto her laptop one more time, and one more time she stared at the words "Mailbox: Empty" on her screen. Then she logged off and reached for her pajamas. She couldn't concentrate on any of her homework. Maybe if she just crawled into bed with a good book, she'd forget about this horrible day. But just as she was snuggling back against her pillow with *The Sisterhood of the Traveling Pants*, the phone rang. She nearly grabbed it, thinking it might be one of the girls, but then she remembered: Simon. It might be him, and she couldn't deal with that right now. He'd called her three times in the last week and e-mailed her, too. Each time the phone rang, she'd let her mom pick it up, holding her breath to see if it would be Simon or not.

"Tell him I'm out with Hannah," she'd whisper.

Her mom had gone along with the Hannah

excuse, the out shopping excuse, and the too much homework excuse. But Nat wasn't sure how much longer her mom would put up with the excuses. So when her mom walked into her bedroom with the portable phone, Nat's heart lurched.

"It's Simon," her mom whispered. "Again."

Nat pulled the pillow over her head. "Can't you tell him I'm washing my hair?" she mumbled.

Her mom frowned. "I've made excuses for you all week. But washing your hair? *That* is where I draw the line."

Nat groaned. "Please. I'll do the dishes for a month. Or a year. Or until I'm forty. I'll—"

"Natalie," her mom said sternly, blocking the receiver with her hand so Simon wouldn't hear. "If you have something to say to Simon, you'd better take the phone and say it now. I won't be your personal answering service anymore." She held out the phone to Nat.

Nat flopped back on her bed and slowly took the phone. Her mom was right. It wasn't like her to blow off anyone—especially someone who'd been as nice to her as Simon had always been. She knew he was calling about the reunion. The problem was that she didn't have the first clue what to say.

"Nat?" Simon said in a relieved voice when Nat finally said hello. "I'm so glad I finally caught you at home!"

"Yeah, I'm sorry I wasn't around this week," Nat said nervously. "I've been super-busy."

"I know. That's what your mom said. So," he

paused, "did you get the invite to the camp reunion?"

Nat took a deep breath. "Yup, I got it."

"Great!" Simon said. Nat could practically hear him smiling into the phone, which made her feel even worse. "So I'll see you there, right? I mean, we haven't seen each other since you came up to Connecticut. And I . . . I miss you."

Nat gripped her bedspread, her heart racing. Why couldn't she say those words back to him? Why was it that she'd had more fun in the last few weeks with her Manhattan friends than she'd had the last few times she'd seen Simon?

"Um, Simon," she said, swallowing down her nervousness. "I was actually going to call you this week, because I'm not going to be able to go to the camp reunion. I told you I got invited to go skiing with Tori, Alyssa, and some of the other girls from camp? Well, it turns out the ski trip is on the same weekend as the reunion."

The silence on the other end of the line hurt her ears.

"Simon?" she said after a full minute of dead air.

"I'm here," he finally said. "I can't believe everything falls on the same weekend. That's such a bummer."

"I know," Nat said truthfully. She was still upset that she would miss out on seeing Alex, Brynn, and the rest of the girls from bunks 4A and 4C at the reunion. But there was also a part of her—a really big part—that was relieved that she couldn't go. Simon was going to be there, and after blowing him off for the last few weeks, she dreaded the awkwardness that was sure to come when she saw him again.

"Maybe we can see each other after you get back," Simon suggested. "I'll still be in town through Monday. I'm going to stay with all the guys at Blake's family's house in the Hamptons, but we can take the train into the city whenever we want. And if you fly back on Monday sometime, we could get together for a movie or something."

"I can't remember when my return flight is," Nat said hurriedly, which was at least partially true. She knew she landed sometime on Monday afternoon, but she wasn't sure exactly when. "Why don't I check my ticket and let you know?"

"Great!" Simon said, his voice sounding cheerier than it had at any point in their talk so far. "I'd love to see you."

"You too," Nat said, figuring that one little white lie wouldn't do too much harm right now. They talked for a few more minutes, but when Nat hung up, she felt sick about everything.

She posted a note on the blog with a big "Help! Guy trouble!" subject line, and within fifteen minutes, Sarah called and listened thoughtfully as Nat vented.

"I just don't want him to get hurt," Nat said. "I never meant for things to get so screwed up."

"Yeah," Sarah said. "That makes two of us. I've messed things up with Abby, big time."

"What happened?" Nat asked.

She could barely believe it when Sarah told her the whole story of how she'd pretended that she hadn't been invited on the trip, hoping that Abby would never have to find out. Sarah was always so considerate . . . it was the last thing she'd expected to hear from her.

"I've called Abby a bunch of times and left her tons of messages, but I haven't heard a peep from her," Sarah said sadly. "And every time I see her in the hallway at school she races for her class. She won't sit with me at lunch or walk home with me. Nothing."

"I'm so sorry," Nat said. "I thought my problem with Simon was a big deal, but this is worse. What's happening to our group of friends? Everything's falling apart."

"I know," Sarah said. "I've barely talked to Brynn and Alex since we got invited on this ski trip."

"Me neither," Nat said. "And Alex is so levelheaded. I'd love to hear her advice on Simon right now." Nat logged back onto her e-mail and checked the blog. There were messages from Jenna, Alyssa, and Grace, all telling her to hang in there. But that was it. "The only girls who have responded to my blog so far are coming skiing."

"Um, Nat?" Sarah said. "That's the other reason I was calling. I already talked to Tori, and I'm about to send out an e-mail to everyone, but I . . . I'm canceling my ticket for the ski trip. I'm going to the reunion instead. It's the only way I can think of to make everything up to Abby."

Nat gripped the phone. "That's such a nice thing you're doing for her," she finally said, trying to hide her disappointment. "But where are you going to stay for the reunion? You know none of the girls can stay in my apartment like I promised. That's a whole other crisis I'm dealing with right now."

"I know," Sarah said. "I'm going to call Brynn and talk to her right now. I think she's trying to figure it out with Priya and Valerie. And Andie, Mia, Becky, and a few of the other counselors are trying to help, too."

"Do me a favor?" Nat asked. "Tell Brynn how sorry I am."

"Sure," Sarah said. "I tried getting ahold of her earlier, but her mom told me she was at rehearsal. Did you know she's playing Eliza in *My Fair Lady* at her school? I had no idea, but I guess she's been putting in some serious rehearsal time lately. And her mom said that Alex is going to see her on opening night next week."

"Oh, wow, Brynn didn't tell me, either." Nat's stomach sunk. She couldn't remember the last time she'd talked to Brynn, and she felt awful that she hadn't known. "That's great! Tell her congrats for me."

"I will," Sarah said, "but I'm sure she'd love to hear it from you, too."

"I doubt it," Nat said. "I e-mailed her a few times, but I haven't heard back."

"Do what I'm going to do with Abby," Sarah said. "Keep trying."

"I will," Nat said.

After she hung up, Nat tossed and turned in bed, trying to sleep, but thoughts kept crowding into her head. She knew Sarah was right. It was up to all of them, now, to make sure their friendships made it through all of this. And that was what worried her more than anything.

Brynn recited her lines one more time as Melanie, Mrs. Callaway's assistant, put the finishing touches on her stage makeup.

"You look great," Melanie said, standing back to look over Brynn's Eliza Doolittle outfit.

Brynn looked at herself in the mirror. Melanie had smudged her cheeks and nose with black face paint to make it look like she was sooty from the London streets. Her petticoats, lace-up shoes, and flower girl hat were perfect. She didn't just look like Eliza Doolittle; she *was* Eliza Doolittle. The opening night for *My Fair Lady* was here, and she was dressed and ready to go. She'd nailed every one of her lines during the dress rehearsal last night, and she'd been practicing them between classes, at lunch, at the dinner table, and even in the shower—she was as ready now as she'd ever be. Her costume was great, the sets were awesome, and every seat in the house was sold out. She would have been totally thrilled, if she wasn't so upset. Where were Alex and Tanya? They'd said they were going to check outside the auditorium one more time before curtain call, but they hadn't come backstage yet.

Brynn waved Mrs. Callaway over.

"Are you ready?" Mrs. Callaway asked. "You're going to be wonderful."

"I hope so," Brynn said. "But can I check the audience one more time?"

Mrs. Callaway sighed. "I'm sure your friend's just

running late, dear, that's all." But at Brynn's pleading look, she added, "All right. Just one more time, but make sure no one sees you."

"Thank you!" Brynn called, already racing to the stage door. She cracked open the door to a slit and peered out at the audience. There were her mom and dad, and three empty seats next to them for Alex, Tanya, and Jordan. But there was no sign of Jordan. And even though Brynn was hoping Grace might just magically show up, too, she knew that was impossible. Grace didn't even know she'd gotten the part of Eliza, or when the play was. Brynn had kept her in the dark about the whole thing, so there was no way Grace would come. Brynn had wanted it that way before, but now she was starting to regret it.

Brynn bit her lip, willing herself to calm down, and when she turned around she practically smacked right into Alex and Tanya.

"Did you find him?" Brynn asked anxiously.

"No," Alex said, "but I'm sure he's on his way."

"Yeah, he promised you he'd be here, right?" Tanya asked.

Brynn nodded, but she felt as if she might burst into tears at any minute. "He's not coming," she managed to whisper.

"Sure he is," Alex said, squeezing her hand. "Hey, I was late getting here, too. My train was way delayed. Maybe Jordan's parents are stuck in traffic or something."

"On a Saturday night?" Brynn said skeptically.

"Did you try calling Priya?" Tanya suggested.

"Maybe she was able to get ahold of him."

"She's on vacation with her family in Michigan this whole week, then flying from there straight to the reunion on Friday," Brynn said. "But before she left she said he was definitely planning on coming to the play. What if he changed his mind? What if he doesn't want to see me perform?"

Tanya and Alex gave each other a look, and then both of them rolled their eyes at Brynn.

"Please," Alex said. "We all saw how nuts he was about you over the summer. There's no way he'd miss this."

"Places, everyone!" Mrs. Callaway called, clapping her hands. "Curtain goes up in two minutes!" She motioned Brynn over to the flower market set, where everyone was getting ready for the opening scene.

"It's time," Brynn said, suddenly having a hard time breathing.

"Stop worrying about Jordan," Alex said. "Get out there and give a Tony-worthy performance."

"He'll be waiting with a dozen roses by the final act," Tanya said. "Trust us."

Brynn took a deep breath, put on her best theatrical smile, and gave them both hugs.

"Thanks so much for coming, Alex," she said. "It means so much to me."

"No problem," Alex said with a grin. "Just remember, when I play in the soccer championship next fall, it's your turn to watch me."

"You know it," Brynn said.

Tanya hugged her one more time. "Break a leg out there. Just make sure it's someone else's," she said, making Brynn laugh.

Brynn watched her two friends take their seats, and then took her place on the set. The band struck up the music, the curtain rose, and a spotlight flashed down on Brynn. As she spoke her opening lines, she lost sight of the audience in the bright stage lights, but she hoped that somewhere out there, Jordan was watching.

Each act flew by, and much faster than Brynn ever thought possible, she was acting out her final scene with Professor Higgins and the audience was bursting into loud applause.

Brynn led all of the players in several stage bows, basking in the glow of the bright lights and the audience's cheers. She could have stayed like that forever, but finally Mrs. Callaway ushered everyone offstage to change out of their costumes.

"Brynn, you were fabulous!" she said, giving her a hug.

Even Lindsay—shocker—offered a very gracious congratulations. "Yeah, you really were a great Eliza," she said. "You were the right choice for the part."

"Thanks," Brynn said, blushing. She changed quickly and, instead of enjoying the backstage celebration with the other actors, she rushed out the theater door and into the throng of people leaving the auditorium. Alex, Tanya, and her mom and dad were all waiting for her with huge smiles.

"Bravo! Bravo!" Tanya shouted, wrapping Brynn

in a huge bear hug.

"You were fantastic!" Alex said.

"I didn't overdo the accent?" Brynn asked.

"No way," Alex said. "I actually forgot you were American, you sounded so much like a Brit."

Brynn beamed as her dad laid a dozen white roses in her arms.

"Flowers for our blooming actress," her mom said, hugging her.

Brynn tried to look as happy as she knew she should be, but when she noticed Alex and Tanya looking everywhere around the auditorium *except* at her, she knew right away. Jordan had never shown up.

"Mom, Dad," she said. "Could you guys bring me some water and food from the reception table? I'm so thirsty, and starving, too." She was hoping they'd take the cue and give her a minute alone with her friends.

"Of course," her mom said, taking her dad by the arm. "We'll be back in a few."

Once they'd gone, Brynn turned to her friends. "I can't believe he didn't come."

"I'm sure he had a really good reason," Alex said. "He probably already left three messages on your voicemail."

Brynn pulled her cell phone out of her purse, but no messages popped up. She shook her head. "I can't believe this."

"Don't jump to any conclusions yet," Tanya said. "Wait until you hear from him."

A single tear slipped out of Brynn's eyes, even though she'd been willing herself not to cry. "I don't know, guys," she said. "Between Jordan and the whole camp reunion disaster, I don't feel like I know who my friends are at all anymore."

"Yeah you do," Alex said. "Us. We'll always be your friends, no matter what. And the other Lakeview girls love you, too. Things are just a little messed up right now, but we'll work them out. At least we found a hotel to stay in for the reunion next weekend."

Brynn nodded. "That's true."

"And you've still got another five performances to go with *My Fair Lady*," Tanya reminded her. "Maybe Jordan will come to one of the other ones this week since he missed this one."

"Maybe," Brynn said, brightening.

"Now," Tanya said. "What are we going to do to celebrate your first standing ovation ever?"

"How about some big, fat banana splits and some Audrey Hepburn movies at my house?" Brynn asked as her parents reappeared.

"Sounds like the perfect plan," Alex said. "And maybe you want to post a note on the camp blog to let everyone know you're on your way to Broadway?"

Brynn hesitated. She knew Alex was trying to play the peacemaker between her and Nat, but Brynn wasn't quite ready to go there—not yet. "I'll tell everyone when we see them next Friday," she decided.

"But what about the girls who won't be there?" Alex asked. "I'm sure they'd love to hear about the play."

Brynn shrugged. She knew she'd have to face that sooner or later, but right now she just wanted to deal with one thing at a time, and Jordan's mysterious no-show was at the top of her list. "I'll tell them, too, when I'm ready."

Alex opened her mouth like she was going to give another convincing argument, but then stopped. "Grace is going to be floored when she finds out." She giggled. "Everyone is going to be so proud of you."

"I hope so," Brynn said. But what she was wishing, more than anything, was that Jordan had been there tonight to be proud of her, too.

chapter SEVEN

Tori ran through her mental list one more time. *Aired out the condo . . . check. Made the bunk beds and cleaned the loft . . . double-check. Went grocery shopping for every kind of food known to mankind . . . check. Heated the Jacuzzi . . . check.* Her parents had agreed to excuse her from school on Friday, just this once. The three of them had arrived at the Tahoe condo earlier that afternoon, and she and her mom had spent every second since then working to get everything ready.

Ever since Sarah had canceled her ticket, Tori felt like the pressure was on, big-time. She wanted to make sure the four girls who were coming skiing had the time of their lives. Because if they didn't, they'd be wishing that they'd gone to the reunion instead, just like Sarah.

Now she waited anxiously at the gate as passengers from Grace's flight deplaned. It seemed like it was taking forever for Grace to appear, but then Tori caught sight of a mass of bright red curls bobbing through the crowd of passengers, and there was Grace, waving like crazy.

"It's so good to see you!" Grace squealed as she

hugged Tori. "I can't believe I'm here! The mountains looked so amazing from the plane. I've never seen mountains that tall in my life."

Tori laughed. "Just wait until you ski down them."

"That's going to be awesome," Grace said as they walked toward the baggage claim. "What time are the other girls coming?"

"They land around six tonight," Tori said. "But you can relax in the condo and unpack. We'll all be together by dinnertime."

Grace clapped her hands excitedly. "I can't wait to see them! I wonder if Nat will have the scoop on what's new with everybody."

Tori laughed. "Probably. She already told me some news she heard from Sarah. Brynn got the leading role in *My Fair Lady*. The last performance was Thursday. Brynn totally kept it a secret this whole time." As soon as the words left her mouth, Tori regretted them. She watched Grace's face fall.

"She was Eliza?" Grace said quietly. "She never mentioned anything to me. I knew she had an audition, but she never told me whether or not she got the part, so I just assumed she hadn't. I've barely talked to her lately. I would've gone to see her . . ." She blinked rapidly, looking like she was about to cry.

Tori could've kicked herself for opening her big mouth. She gave Grace's arm a gentle squeeze. "I'm sure she was going to tell you. She probably just forgot."

Grace stared at the luggage as it rolled past them on the baggage carousel. "Maybe," she said. "I'll have to call her to find out how it went. We used to talk a lot, but now . . ." Her voice died away and she looked up guiltily at Tori.

"I know." Tori sighed. "Everything's screwed up."

"No, not everything!" Grace said, trying to be more positive. "We're getting to spend the weekend together, and it's going to be a blast." She smiled. "I'm really glad I came on this trip, Tori, no matter what."

"Thanks," Tori said. "I'm glad you still feel that way." She took a deep breath. "Now, let's get your stuff and get back to the condo so that we can eat. Are you hungry?"

"Starving," Grace said.

"Good." As they drove back to the condo, the two of them talked and laughed and sang songs along with the radio, and Tori started to feel a little better. Things may not have worked out exactly like she'd hoped, but maybe this weekend could still be amazing anyway.

▲ ▲ ▲

Any way Sarah looked at it, the reunion weekend was off to an awful start. As planned, she stepped off the train at Penn Station on Friday night to meet the rest of the girls a full day ahead of the official camp reunion and get a head start on the fun. She was sure she'd be able to fix everything with Abby as soon as she got to New York. But nothing had gone according to her plans.

Mia, the CIT from Bunk 4A and one of the

chaperones for the weekend, had picked her up from the station alone—no Abby in tow. While all the other Lakeview girls were ecstatic to see Sarah, and the counselors who were chaperoning at the hotel—Andie, Becky, and Sophie—gave her huge hugs, too, Abby stayed hidden in the room she was sharing with Priya and Valerie.

"You're rooming with me and Brynn," Alex had explained to Sarah. "Mia had you and Abby listed as roommates when we all first got here, but . . ." She shrugged awkwardly. "Abby's still pretty upset."

"Oh," Sarah said, her heart sinking. "Okay." She tried to smile brightly, not wanting to make Alex or Brynn feel bad. But she'd been hoping against hope that maybe Abby had requested a room with her earlier in the day. No such luck.

Now she was suffering through what was supposed to be a fab Thai dinner with her camp friends, but was more like a doom and gloom disaster. This was their first big night on the town; they'd gotten discount tickets to see the Off Broadway show *Stomp!* after dinner. But even with all the great stuff the counselors had planned for them, none of the girls seemed to be having a good time.

Abby had chosen to sit at the end of the table farthest away from Sarah. Every time Sarah tried to make eye contact with her, Abby made a point of looking the other way. Priya tried to get a good conversation going by talking about Riley, her new crush at home, but nobody seemed all that interested. And Valerie tried to liven things up by reading *Teen* magazine's "50

Most Embarrassing Celeb Moments" out loud while everyone ate, but nobody giggled, even a little, at one of J-Lo's wardrobe malfunctions.

"I think this will be the first time I've eaten food I can identify with Lakeview campers," Sarah said, trying to lighten the mood.

It seemed to work momentarily, because Alex giggled. "That's one of my favorite parts of the reunion. As Nat would say, it's Camp Lakeview without the Lakepuke part."

A few of the other girls laughed, too, but Sarah noticed that at the mention of Nat's name, some of the light blinked out in their eyes.

"Nat can be such a prima donna sometimes," Chelsea snipped. "We're lucky she's not here. And the other girls in Tahoe for that matter, too. We don't need them."

Karen stared at her plate, looking close to tears. "But it's not the same without them."

"Yeah," Alex said. "I was just thinking how weird it was not to have to wait for Nat and Tori to get ready tonight. They always take forever, painting their nails and fixing their hair." She sighed. "Even though it's a pain sometimes, I kind of miss it right now."

"Me too," Brynn said softly. "And I could totally use some of Nat's advice on guys right now, too. I tried calling Jordan three times since the play closed yesterday, but all I got was his voicemail."

"I haven't heard from him since before I left on vacation," Priya said. "Something's definitely up with that boy, and I'm kind of worried."

Brynn sighed. "I'm really worried, too, but I'm also really annoyed."

"I don't blame you," Abby piped up. "It *is* annoying when someone you care about blows you off."

And with that, Abby got up and headed for the restrooms, leaving Sarah turning several shades redder than the curry chicken on her plate.

"I'm sure she didn't mean that," Valerie said.

"She so did, but I probably deserved it," Sarah said, standing up. What if Abby went the whole weekend without speaking to her? Talk about awkward. No, but that wouldn't happen. It couldn't. Sarah would make sure of that. "I need to talk to her—now. Wish me luck. I'm gonna need it."

But she didn't need luck. She needed a miracle. So she waited for Abby in the quiet hallway outside the restrooms. When Abby saw her, she just frowned and tried to step around her, but Sarah blocked her way.

"Can we please talk for a minute?" Sarah pleaded. "It's going to be hard to avoid me for the whole weekend."

Abby just stood there, silently. The tension grew until it was so thick, Sarah almost caved. "You have two minutes," Abby finally said, just in the nick of time.

"Abs," Sarah started, "I'm so, so, so sorry. Did you get all the messages I left for you?"

Abby shrugged. "Maybe, but they don't change the fact that you lied."

"I was completely wrong," Sarah said. "A real jerk. I should've told you the truth from the beginning, but I was scared that you'd be mad at me and hurt that you weren't invited to Tahoe and I was."

Abby glared at her. "But don't you get it? I don't care whether you got invited and I didn't."

"You don't?" Sarah blinked in surprise.

"No," Abby said. "I'm not even that close to Tori, so it makes sense that she wouldn't ask me to come if she could only invite five girls. But I never expected you to lie to me—ever. That's what hurt more than anything."

"I'm sorry," Sarah whispered. "That's why I decided not to go to Tahoe. Because your friendship is way more important to me than a few days of skiing. I wouldn't have had nearly as much fun without you, anyway." She felt like her heart was spilling out into her words, that's how much she meant what she was saying.

Abby gave her a long look, like she was trying to figure out whether Sarah was telling the truth or not. Then, after what seemed like an eternity to Sarah, Abby smiled. A small, hesitant smile—but still, a smile nonetheless.

"From now on," Abby said in a tone that was teasing and serious all at the same time, "no more secrets. Got it?"

"Got it," Sarah said, hugging Abby as she let out a sigh of relief. "Never again. So . . . do you want to bunk with me and Alex and Brynn?"

Abby smiled. "Sure. I'll ask Priya and Val if they want to join us. We can just bring in our pillows and blankets and sleep on the floor."

As the girls left the restaurant for the theater, relief washed over Sarah. And when Abby sat next to her during *Stomp!*, Sarah felt like she had a perma-smile glued to her face. Afterward, she was in such a great mood that not even the fact that the Tahoe girls were MIA could dampen her spirits.

"What an incredible show!" Sarah said as the girls streamed out of the theater doors.

"I can't believe they made real music with trash can lids and brooms," Abby said, flipping through her playbill one more time.

"I could have lived without the trash can lids," Chelsea grumbled. "My ears are still ringing."

"Oh come on, Chelsea," Alex said. "You loved the show, too. Admit it. I looked over at you once in the last half and you were smiling and tapping your feet, just like the rest of us."

"Humph," was all Chelsea could say to that, making Sarah giggle.

The girls were in good spirits as they headed back to the hotel, but once they got there, it seemed to hit them all over again that Jenna wouldn't be playing any midnight pranks, and Nat wouldn't be giving out any spa treatments or sharing in the latest Hollywood gossip. Sarah and Abby stayed up late talking with Brynn and Alex, but the other girls quietly shuffled off to bed. And even though Sarah was so glad that she and Abby had made up, she felt a little frustrated with everyone else. She'd given up Tahoe to come to the reunion, and now she wanted to have a great time while she was here. As she drifted off to sleep, she made a silent wish that over the course of the weekend, everyone would forget who was missing from the group and remember who was there to have a great time.

"Bombs away!" a gleeful voice yelled into the darkness, and before Nat had a clue what was happening, a shower of snowballs pummeled down on her.

She brushed the bitter cold snow off her face and jacket and struggled to catch her breath through giggles. When she finally did, she shouted, "Jenna Bloom, you are so going to pay for that!"

Alyssa gathered up some fresh ammunition. She handed a pile of firmly packed snowballs to Nat, then whispered, "You distract them while I sneak up behind them. They'll never know what hit them."

Nat watched Alyssa slither on her belly over the snowbank they were using as a barricade, and then wound up her arm to launch an attack on the enemy. As soon as Nat, Jenna, and Alyssa had gotten to the condo, the girls had eaten and then headed outside for a moonlit snowball war. It had been Jenna's idea, since everyone—even Tori—had been unusually quiet during dinner. Nat guessed they were all thinking the same thing—that they were three thousand miles away from the rest of their friends who, at this very moment, were all getting together for pre-reunion girl-bonding.

Even though Tori's condo was completely fab, and Tahoe was breathtaking with its soaring mountains and crisp, clean snow, the reality of the reunion was sinking in.

Nat catapulted another snowball and then leaped over the snowbank with a warrior cry, firing the rest of the snowballs in rapid succession right at the fallen tree trunk that Grace, Tori, and Jenna were hiding behind. She ran full force toward the trunk, and in the bright moonlight she could see the looks of surprise on the girls' faces. But they were about to get an even bigger surprise. Because just as Nat reached them from the front, Alyssa crept up on them from behind and dumped huge handfuls of snow right down the back of Jenna's jacket.

"Cold cold cold!" Jenna gasped, trying to scoop the snow off her neck. "Somebody help me!"

But Tori and Grace were way too busy laughing to be of any help.

"Justice has been served," Alyssa said, high-fiving Nat.

"Man, if Alex were here right now," Jenna said, "we'd cream you guys. We'd—" Suddenly she stopped, glancing guiltily at Tori. "Sorry," she said quietly.

"Hey, no biggie. It's not like we can't talk about the other girls." Tori shrugged, but as carefully as she was trying to hide it, Nat could tell she felt bad.

"I don't know about you guys," Nat piped up, searching for a subject change, "but I think I'm starting to get brain freeze out here. Maybe we could hit the Jacuzzi for a while?"

"Definitely!" Tori said, a little too enthusiastically. "Or I could have my mom go into town to rent us some DVDs. Or if that doesn't sound good, I brought tons of games and CDs. We could burn some tunes for our iPods. We could go night skiing, too, but we'd have to rent our skis tonight, and it'd be really cold. But—"

Alyssa held up her hands. "Whoa! Time out! You're starting to sound like one of those radio announcers who talks a hundred miles a minute." She smiled. "I vote with Nat on the Jacuzzi. That sounds toasty."

Everyone nodded, and they shook the remaining snow off their jackets and jeans before heading inside. The sweet smell of hot chocolate hit Nat's nose as soon as she stepped over the threshold, and she saw a tray of steaming cups loaded with marshmallows set out on the living room coffee table next to a roaring fire.

"I thought you girls might need a little warming up," Tori's mom said.

"I wasn't sure what you guys would like, so if you don't want hot chocolate," Tori said, "there's OJ, soda, tea, apple juice, and some V-8s, too."

"What, no bug juice?" Jenna asked with a serious look.

Nat could see she was teasing, but Tori immediately flushed with worry. "Um, you know, I didn't see anything like it at the store. I don't even know what it's called in real life."

Jenna put a hand on Tori's arm. "Hey, I was just kidding around. Bug juice outside of camp—ick."

Tori giggled nervously. "Oh, right. Ick."

"Hot chocolate sounds delish," Nat said, and they each took a cup and then trooped upstairs to change into their bathing suits while Tori helped her mom clean up the dinner dishes.

Once they were safely in the condo's loft, Nat whispered, "Is it just me, or does Tori seem a little . . . nervous?"

"Totally," Jenna said, and Alyssa nodded, too. "She's making me uptight just watching her. Major overkill on the whole hostess thing."

"She's been like that since I got here this afternoon," Grace said. "I forgot my camera, and she told her mom to go out and buy me a disposable one. We'd barely gotten in the front door and her mom had to turn around and go right back into town. I felt awful about it, but Tori wouldn't take no for an answer. And it wasn't even a big deal."

"I guess she just wants to make sure we're having a good time," Alyssa said.

Jenna pulled out her cell phone, checked the screen, and then flopped back on her bunk with a sigh. "I haven't heard a peep from Alex yet. I'm sure she's with the other girls in New York by now."

Grace sunk down on her bed, looking gloomy. "I don't think they want to talk to us. Brynn didn't even tell me she got the part of Eliza in her school play. I'm dying to call her, but I feel funny doing it in front of Tori. I don't want to make her feel like I'm not having a good time out here."

"Don't you wonder what everyone's doing in Manhattan, though?" Nat asked. She'd been thinking about it all day, and even though she was relieved that she didn't have to see Simon just yet, she was missing the whole feeling of camp togetherness she felt last year at the reunion.

Alyssa nodded. "I bet they're doing something great tonight."

"I know this sounds awful," Jenna said in a low voice, "because it's so beautiful here, and I'm sure we're going to have a fab time. But I sort of wish I'd gone to the reunion instead."

All the girls fell quiet, and Nat could tell they were all thinking the same thought—what a bummer it was to be missing the reunion and missing the rest of their friends. There was no way any of them could let Tori know that, though. For now, they'd just have to make the best of the weekend and try to forget about the reunion, which would be easier said than done.

▲　▲　▲

Brynn thought she understood what the word "posh" meant, but that was before she walked into Tiffany & Co. The crinkled, grease-dotted bag of Krispy Kreme doughnuts Andie was carrying looked completely out of place next to the glittering jewelry that filled the squeaky-clean showcases.

"Okay," Andie said, opening the bag, "who wants their *Breakfast at Tiffany's?*"

"I'm in," Brynn said, grabbing a chocolate doughnut from the stack and blatantly ignoring the pompous scowl one of the salesclerks was giving her. "We must do as Audrey Hepburn did in the movie, every step of the way."

"I've never seen the movie, but I also *never* pass up a doughnut." Abby grinned, digging her hand into the bag.

"I can't eat," Karen said in a hushed tone. "I'm afraid I'll get sugar all over the floor."

"This was such a dumb idea," Chelsea added. "Audrey Hepburn ate outside Tiffany's while she looked in the windows. She didn't go *inside*. How embarrassing is this?"

"It's so much more realistic this way, though," Brynn said between mouthfuls of yummy sweetness. It had been her idea to eat breakfast on Saturday at Tiffany & Co. in honor of Audrey Hepburn (one of her all-time favorite actresses), and she was going to make the most of it, even if everyone else was still in a foul mood because they missed the girls in Tahoe. She still hadn't heard from Jordan, either, so she needed something to cheer herself up, and she thought this might do the trick. She'd even bought herself a pair of Jackie O'–style sunglasses to wear and put her hair up in a twist that morning, just like Holly Golightly wore it in the movie.

As she finished up her last bite of doughnut, she slid her favorite mood ring off her finger. "Watch this," she said to Sarah, Abby, and Alex, then sauntered over to a counter where a stuffy-looking clerk was carefully arranging some displays of diamond necklaces.

"Can I help you, miss?" he said, keeping a watchful eye on how close Brynn came to the glass case.

Brynn smiled and said, in her best imitation of Audrey Hepburn, "Yes, please, sir. I'm wondering if I could have this engraved?" She held out her mood ring, ignoring the muffled giggles from the girls behind her.

The clerk, whose nametag read PERCY, rolled his eyes. "Let me guess. You've seen the movie a dozen times?"

"Three dozen," Brynn said proudly. "To be exact."

"Well, miss, *to be exact*, we don't engrave merchandise from other stores. My apologies."

Brynn kept smiling, a new wave of determination sweeping through her. "Do you think you could make an exception, just this once? My friends and I are only in town for the weekend, and it would be the best souvenir I've ever gotten."

Percy looked over Brynn's shoulder at the other girls, who were all watching expectantly, holding their breaths.

"Oh, all right, if I must," Percy said, taking the mood ring from Brynn. "You can pick it up later this afternoon."

"Yes!" Brynn cried. "Thank you so much. I'd like it to say *Lakeview Reunion*. And . . . will you put it in the little blue Tiffany's box for me, too?"

At that moment, she thought she saw Percy's lips twitch upward ever so slightly into a quarter-smile, but he caught himself before it grew bigger.

"Very well," he said. "Now, if you'll excuse me, I have an important client to attend to." He nodded over his shoulder to an elderly woman in a mink coat wearing some serious bling bling and scrutinizing the merchandise for her next purchase.

"Thanks so much, Perc," Brynn said.

"You're welcome," he muttered, then before turning away, added, "And please tell your little friends not to touch *anything* in the store."

Brynn thanked him again and then turned back to the girls, hoping that everyone would be laughing. But even her performance didn't bring a smile to most of their faces. Only Alex, Sarah, Abby, and the counselors were quietly applauding.

"You are crazy!" Abby said, high-fiving her.

"That might have even topped your Eliza Doolittle," Alex added. "It's a close call."

Brynn shrugged. "What can I say? I'm a sucker for Audrey. So, where should we go while we're waiting for my ring to be finished?"

"We could go to Saks, or Barneys?" Mia suggested.

"It doesn't matter to me," Priya said, and Valerie added, "Me neither."

But Brynn, Sarah, Abby, and Alex all voted for Barneys. "I don't know if we can top Tiffany's, but we can try," Brynn said. And as it turned out, what Tiffany's did for jewelry, Barneys did for fashion. Even Brynn was afraid to touch some of the gorgeous tops and skirts draped elegantly on hanger after hanger. But the other girls were less than enthused by the fab clothes. Priya, Valerie, Chelsea, and Karen found some plush couches outside one of the dressing rooms and sat down, glumly thumbing through magazines.

At least Alex was brave enough to try on a few velvety pageboy caps that didn't cost a fortune, but when it came to choosing between a heather gray color or cranberry, no one had any helpful advice for her.

"You know who the fashion queens are," Chelsea said, "and they're busy skiing."

"But I can't pick!" Alex cried. Just then, Alex's phone rang and she gave up on the hats for a second to pick it up.

"Saved by the cell," Sarah said, heading for the shoe department with Abby and Brynn while Alex talked. "Should we try on some Manolo Blahniks just for fun?" she asked, picking up a strappy black stiletto.

"Manolo Blankets? What are they?" Abby asked blankly, making Brynn giggle.

"They're the crème de la crème of shoes," Brynn said, grabbing a pair of satiny crimson kitten heels off the display rack. But within seconds, a saleswoman in a tailored suit descended on her, delicately plucking the shoes out of her hands.

"Excuse me, ladies," she said, "but I don't believe we carry these in your size."

Brynn resisted the urge to glare at the woman. What was with the stuck-up customer service in these stores? "We don't want them anyway," Brynn said, raising her chin aloofly as she sashayed away in Alex's direction. "They don't make them like they used to."

She and Sarah and Abby broke into giggles, but when they saw Alex's sober face, their laughter died away.

"What's wrong?" Brynn asked her.

"That was Adam," Alex said. "He was calling to see what we were up to. They just left Blake's house in the Hamptons to come into the city. I guess they're going to South Street Seaport for a while before the reunion." She looked sheepishly at Brynn. "But . . . he told me that Jordan never showed up. And their counselor Kenny hasn't heard from him, and neither have any of the other counselors."

"Oh," was all Brynn could say. After trying so hard all morning to lift everyone else's spirits, she suddenly felt drained of all ability to smile, laugh, or do anything remotely fun. She'd almost managed to stop thinking about Jordan in their morning shopping excursion, but now her funk was back in a big way.

"Hey," Sarah said. "It's still early. He still has time to show for the reunion."

"And I bet he'll have a great excuse for everything," Abby said.

Brynn nodded, but between Alex's news and the depressing vibes radiating from the other girls, she'd had enough. Why should she make the effort to stay in a good mood when her boyfriend had ditched her and half her friends were three thousand miles away?

When Mia and Andie said it was time to grab some lunch and then head back to the hotel to get ready for the reunion, Brynn quietly followed everyone out of the store. She barely even noticed when Mia slipped her arm around her.

"I'm sure he'll get in touch when he can," she said, "and in the meantime, we can pick up your mood ring from Tiffany's after lunch. That might put the smile back on your face, huh?"

Brynn nodded, but she knew her smile was gone, maybe for the rest of the day. If she'd had her mood ring on right now, there was no doubt what color it would be: a deep, depressing black.

chapter

NINE

Tori knew the girls were miserable, and it wasn't even one o'clock in the afternoon yet. If she'd known that a blizzard was going to hit Tahoe on Saturday, she would have planned a trip to the tropics instead. But as it was, they were stuck trying to ski in a howling storm, and Tori's vision of palm trees and warm beaches were fading in the face of subzero temps and blinding snow.

They'd woken up to a beautiful blanket of fresh powder and had rented their equipment and hit the slopes for ski lessons, but soon the innocent-looking snowflakes had turned into pelting bullets of ice. Since the mountain was still open, except the top of the peak because of wind conditions, the girls were still making an effort. But this was so not the glamorous West Coast skiing Tori'd envisioned for her friends.

She watched with a sinking heart as Nat fell (again) and slid halfway down the mountain on her backside. Heidi, their ski instructor, rushed to help while Tori retrieved Nat's scattered poles and one of her skis from the side of the run.

"Maybe I'm not cut out for this," Nat mumbled

to Tori through chattering teeth.

"It just takes practice," Tori said.

Alyssa, Jenna, and Grace half skied, half wobbled over then, looking just as frozen as Tori felt.

"You guys okay?" Tori said.

"What?" Alyssa cried over the howling wind as she clung to her poles like she was hanging on for dear life. "I can barely hear you. You've got your scarf wrapped so tightly around your face that all I can see is your nose."

"As for me, I think my eyelashes just froze together," Jenna said, waving a gloved hand in front of her face in mock panic.

Tori had to hand it to Jenna for trying to joke in the midst of everything. And Tori wanted to laugh at that, really she did. But since she couldn't feel her lips or her cheeks, laughing was out of the question. Her toes, her fingers, her legs, her arms—she was pretty sure that every single part of her body was absolutely, completely numb.

"Hey," Grace said, "what does it feel like when you have frostbite?"

Alyssa examined a frozen strand of her hair that had turned completely white with ice crystals where it wasn't covered by her hat. "I don't think you can feel frostbite, because you lose all feeling in the parts of your body that are affected."

Tori sighed. They'd only been in their lesson for a little over an hour, but everyone—herself included—was having an awful time. "Do you guys want to take a break?"

"No, this is f-f-f-f-f-un," Grace stammered, shivering so badly that her skis clacked together.

"Yeah, I want to keep trying," Nat said, grunting as she struggled to snap her boots into her skis again. "These things are definitely *not* made for comfort. I feel like I've got a pair of two-by-fours for feet." She tried a smile, but it fell flat. But then she must have seen the concern in Tori's eyes, because she suddenly shifted into her typical Nat cheeriness. "I'll get the hang of it soon, I'm sure. Let's go!"

Nat motioned for the other girls to take the lead, and Tori made it down to the bottom first. Jenna, Alyssa, and Grace came down slowly, fighting the wind and swirling snow, but they made it after a few minutes. Nat was a different story entirely.

"Hey," Jenna said, pointing to where Nat was sliding down the hill in a cloud of powder behind Heidi, "does creating an avalanche count as skiing?"

"Wait a sec," Tori said, panic rising inside her, "doesn't she look like she's going to—"

"Heidi, look out!" Alyssa shouted, but it was too late. Screaming at the top of her lungs, Nat smacked into Heidi, and their skis popped off and went flying while they tumbled to a stop at the foot of the hill.

"Oh, man." Jenna let out a whistle. "Let's go see if there are survivors. I'd make a joke, but I think my sense of humor just froze."

"Are you guys all right?" Tori asked, skiing over as Heidi slowly got to her feet.

"Oh, I'm fine." Heidi said, but Tori noticed her smile was drooping for the first time since the lesson started. "It's one of the hazards of my job. Why do you think I wear ski pants with an extra layer of padding in them?"

Nat, on the other hand, wasn't even trying to smile anymore. In fact, she looked like she might start crying any minute. "Now I know I'm destined to be a metropolitan girl forever," she grumbled. "Ice-skating in Central Park I could handle, but this . . . is ridiculous." As soon as the words left her mouth, she gasped. "Oh, Tori, I'm sorry! I didn't mean that. I'm just a total grump in serious need of a heating pad, that's all. I'm having a great time . . . really."

"Not a prob," Tori said, masking the quivering in her voice with fake cheeriness. She was glad her eyes had been watering all day from the bitter wind, because now no one would notice the real tears pricking her eyes. "This isn't my idea of fun, either," she went on, deciding it was best to act like she was laughing the whole thing off. "Not only am I in danger of losing my fingers, which would make me miss out on manicures for the rest of my life, but for all I know, my toes might already be turning black inside my boots. I vote we call it quits for the day and go thaw out."

"Are you sure?" Grace asked. "We really don't mind staying . . ."

"Yep," Tori said. "It's way too frigid out here." She wracked her brain to come up with a Plan B, desperate to find a way to keep her friends entertained and their minds off the reunion. Then it came to her. "I say we go back to the condo, get changed, and then go out for an early dinner. There's a great place called the Overlook that has karaoke, and they have the best hot chocolate in town."

"Anywhere indoors sounds good to me," Alyssa said.

The girls made plans to reschedule the rest of their lesson with Heidi for Sunday morning, and then slowly dragged themselves to the condo to regroup. Tori put on a happy face, but she knew in her heart that no matter how hard she tried, this trip wasn't going to be as much fun as the reunion—not even close.

▲ ▲ ▲

"Come on, you guys! I want to get out there sometime this millennium!" Sarah called over her shoulder as she finished lacing up her ice skates. Skyscrapers surrounded the rink and the rest of Central Park. The late Saturday afternoon sunshine was glinting off their windows, tinting the whole city with an orange glow. It was a beautiful day for a camp reunion.

The Camp Lakeview alma mater was blaring from the speakers around the skating rink, and the ice was filling with groups of campers. There was David, hanging onto the wall of the rink with Adam, Blake, Simon, and Devon. He was already waving Sarah over, and she felt like she couldn't hit the ice fast enough. They'd been e-mailing each other, but the last time they'd actually seen each other had been right before Sarah got invited on the ski trip. And now she couldn't wait to spend some time with him (and kick his butt in the Ice Capades, too, of course).

"They're such slowpokes," Abby mumbled

to Sarah, nodding to the rest of the girls who were pulling on their skates with about as much enthusiasm as a bunch of snails. Andie and Mia had made sure that all the girls were wearing sweatshirts in their Color War colors for the skating games. Half of them were decked out in red and the other half in blue. As soon as Sarah pulled on her sweatshirt, a familiar rush pumped through her veins.

She loved a good competition, and tonight she and Abby were ready to take on the other bunks in whatever types of games Dr. Steve had planned. But she and Abby seemed like the only ones out of the 4As and 4Cs who had one ounce of enthusiasm. Chelsea was already griping about her feet hurting, and Brynn hadn't even touched her skates yet. Instead, she was scouring every inch of the rink with her eyes, looking for Jordan.

"No sign of him yet?" Sarah asked her quietly, and all Brynn could do was shake her head as her eyes became glassy.

"I don't even feel like skating anymore," she said. "You guys go ahead without me."

Sarah couldn't believe what she was hearing. There was no way she was going to let Brynn back out of the reunion plans that easily, especially when just this morning Brynn had been taking Manhattan (and Tiffany's) by storm. "Cheer up, girly," Sarah tried, pulling Brynn to her feet. "I know you miss Jordan, but you can't mope all night."

Brynn sighed, but reluctantly followed Sarah, Alex, and Abby onto the ice to meet the guys.

"Wow," Alex whispered as they skated over to them, "They look pretty funny on ice skates, don't they?"

Sarah tried not to giggle too loudly, but it was true. Devon and Blake were the only guys who looked steady on their skates. Adam and David were wobbling shakily, their ankles bent awkwardly inward. But Sarah really broke into laughter when David tried to give her a hug and nearly toppled over.

"I think you might need to give me some ice-skating lessons before I let go," David told her, still clutching the wall for balance.

Sarah held out her hand to him. "I don't know," she teased. "I might have to wait to give you tips until after we beat you in the Ice Capades."

She whooped and cheered as Dr. Steve skated onto the ice with a bullhorn. The counselors joined him in the center of the rink while dozens of campers gathered around, hugging, laughing, and catching up.

"Ladies and gentlemen," Dr. Steve started, "welcome to the annual Lakeview Camp Reunion! It's great to see all of your smiling faces. I'm glad so many of you could join us. Now, who's ready to have some fun tonight?"

Sarah and Abby burst into loud cheers with most of the other campers, but she noticed that Priya and Valerie could only muster up lousy halfhearted "woo-hoos."

"Glad to hear it," he said. "We're going to start off the night with Lakeview's own version of the Ice Capades. Then maybe a little friendly game of broom hockey."

"Yes!" Sarah heard Blake call out behind her. "You're looking at the hockey king, right here! Get ready to eat my ice!"

Sarah rolled her eyes. Well, Blake hadn't changed much since last summer.

"After you all work up a healthy appetite on the ice," Dr. Steve continued while the counselors set up an obstacle course of tires and cones behind him, "we'll serve you some of our famous mess-hall gruel, courtesy of Pete!" Pete skated forward and took a bow to the resounding "boos" of the entire camp.

"What, you don't like my mystery meat loaf?" Pete asked, pretending to be hurt.

Dr. Steve laughed. "All right, all right, we're just teasing. We're going to the Jekyll & Hyde Club for some monster burgers and mad-scientist elixir."

Everyone cheered, and David leaned over to Sarah and Abby with a wicked smile and whispered in a hilariously bad German accent, "Ah, yes, yes, you haven't met my evil twin, Dr. Dread. By the light of the full moon, I will drink my special potion and transform myself. Mua ha ha ha."

Sarah giggled. She loved David's wacky sense of humor.

"All right!" Dr. Steve said as the Olympic fanfare echoed through the rink. "Let the games begin!"

Sarah linked arms with Abby and Alex to skate over to the 4As and 4Cs section of the ice. "Good luck!" she called to the guys, laughing as David and Adam tried not to lose their balance on the ice.

"You'll need it."

Over the next few hours, Sarah and Abby tore up the ice, acing the obstacle course, but then things started to fall apart. The ice dancing contest (a warped rendition of real ice dancing, where instead of coupling up for ballroom-like dancing, each bunk choreographed their own special bunk-dance routine) was a total disaster for the girls. 4A's rendition of "Ice, Ice, Baby" sounded more like a funeral dirge than pop, and 4C's "Snowbound" didn't sound any better. So the guys completely smoked them there, despite Abby and Brynn's attempt to pull off a last-minute victory with a cool dance move they'd dubbed "The Icewalk" instead of "The Moonwalk." Even after scoring ten goals between them in the broom hockey game, Sarah and Abby couldn't muster up any excitement from the other girls. Sure, Priya and Valerie participated, but it was like they were moving in slow-motion. Even Alex, who was usually in her element when it came to sports, had trouble holding her own as goalie. She let five goals slip past her before throwing down her broom in frustration.

"I am so off my game today," she said. "I don't know what my problem is."

"I know what *my* problem is," Chelsea said. "Blisters. I'm taking a break."

"You can't quit now," Sarah cried as Chelsea skated toward the snack shack. "We're not even halfway through the game."

But Chelsea just kept going. And Karen, after glancing apologetically at Sarah and Abby, skated after her. "Sorry, guys," she called over her shoulder. "But I've already fallen so much that I'm not going to be able to sit for a week."

"Another one bites the dust," Abby said, but no sooner had the words left her mouth than Brynn said, "Guys, I think I'm going to sit the rest of the game out, too."

"But, Brynn, you can't . . ." Sarah started, but when she saw Brynn's trembling lip, she stopped.

"Sorry," Brynn whispered.

"Now what?" Sarah muttered, looking around at the meager team they had left.

"I'm calling an emergency meeting," Andie said, gathering all the girls together in the snack shack. "Who's going to tell me what's going on?"

"Don't ask me," Sarah said, letting her frustration boil over. "I've been trying all afternoon to get everyone to stop moping, but I give up. I cancelled the trip to Tahoe for the reunion, but I'm starting to wonder why. I didn't know I was going to be dealing with a bunch of downers all weekend."

"I second that," Abby said. "I thought camp reunions were supposed to be fun. This is my first one ever and it's like we're all at a funeral or something."

Everyone stared at their feet for a minute before Brynn spoke up.

"It's not just the whole Jordan thing that's got me upset," she said quietly, biting her lip. "I miss Grace. I've barely talked to her at all since the whole Tahoe thing started, but now I feel awful that I haven't. And I can't imagine the rest of this weekend without her."

"Or Nat and Tori, either," Priya piped up. "I don't even think I'd mind if they hogged the bathroom mirrors with all their primping, if they were here."

"And I've never been to a reunion without Jenna," Alex said. "We always team up in sports, but today I can't even stop a goal without her here."

Sarah looked at the sad faces of her friends, wanting more than anything to pull them out of this slump. "Look, guys, I know we miss the rest of the girls. But we can't let it ruin our time together, right?"

"It's not just that we miss them," Valerie said. "It's that things are so tense. We've barely even talked to them lately. That's the worst part."

Priya nodded in agreement. "I'm upset that we didn't all get to go to Tahoe together. But I wouldn't have wanted to miss out on the reunion, anyway. And now it's like Tori, Nat, and the other girls don't even *want* to talk to us, or hang around us anymore."

"I know that's not true," Sarah said. "Before I canceled my ticket to Tahoe, Nat, Jenna, Alyssa, Grace, and I all talked about that. We wanted to talk to you guys, but we felt bad that we were invited and you weren't. We thought you were mad at us."

"We were only mad because no one talked to us about any of it," Karen said. "This wall went up between our two groups, and that was it."

"We can patch things up with them," Sarah said. "It's never too late for that. Maybe we can figure something out at dinner tonight. But right now, we need to focus on *our* time together. I know Jenna would be furious if she knew we were throwing away a chance to kick the boys' butts in this broom hockey game. And Nat would tell us that all this frowning is bad for our complexions."

Andie laughed at that. "Truer words have never been spoken. No one, especially the girls in Tahoe, would want you to be miserable this weekend when you should be having fun."

Slowly, every one of the girls nodded, and a few small smiles even surfaced. Just then, Kenny skated over. "Ladies, the guys are wondering if you're forfeiting the game," he said.

"Forfeiting!" Sarah cried. "They wish!" She turned to her friends. "Who wants to get out there again and totally annihilate them?"

"Count me in," Abby said, grabbing her broom, and soon all the other girls, even Brynn, were heading back onto the ice.

Sarah smiled. She knew they still hadn't fixed the awkwardness with the girls in Tahoe, and she wasn't sure how or when that would happen. But for right now, this was a promising start.

chapter

TEN

Nat sighed as she looked out the huge windows of the Overlook Café at the blustering snow. Her fingers and toes had finally thawed out after this morning's skiing disaster, but even so, her mood hadn't improved much, and neither had anyone else's. Jenna and Alyssa had eaten most of their dinners in silence, and Tori had been talking almost nonstop with a mega-cheeriness that was bordering on hysteria. To top it all off, the girls were listening to some very bad karaoke attempts from other snowed-in skiers who'd called it a day. Normally, operatic renditions of ABBA's "Dancing Queen" would have been funny to watch, but right now, none of the girls were smiling or laughing. The whole day had been one awkward moment after another, and now, as much as she hated to admit it, Nat was wishing that she'd stayed home in Manhattan and gone to the reunion.

As a sixty-year-old man finished up his version of Barry Manilow's "I Can't Smile Without You," Tori burst into hoots and overzealous applause, but she was the only one at their table clapping.

"Okay," she said, smiling way too enthusiastically at the other girls, "who's up next? Jenna, I know you're dying to get up there."

But Jenna just shook her head. "Nah, not today. I'm just not feeling the karaoke calling."

"Me neither," Alyssa said quietly. "My sorry attempt at skiing took it all out of me."

Grace was in the bathroom, so Tori looked expectantly at Nat, and Nat felt guilt settling down deep in her stomach. "Sorry, Tori," Nat said. "I'm too sore to move, let alone sing."

Tori just nodded, but her eyes brimmed with tears. "This was all a big mistake. I should've canceled this whole trip and never asked you to come."

"What are you talking about?" Nat asked.

Tori took a few deep breaths before she could speak again. "You're all having an awful time. I can tell. Grace has been humming some song from *My Fair Lady* since yesterday, so I know she's missing Brynn. And Jenna, you haven't pulled one prank since you've gotten here."

Jenna shrugged. "I guess I just haven't felt much like it."

"Exactly." Tori sighed. "That's the whole problem. Nobody's being themselves. You guys didn't want to come here at all, did you?"

Nat sighed. Great—this was just great. They'd really screwed up this trip now. "Tori," she started, "of course we wanted to come. It's just that . . . we all feel bad about how messed up our friendships with the other girls are right now. But that's totally not your fault."

"Yeah," Jenna jumped in, putting her arm around Tori. "The problem is that none of us handled the situation very well. I never knew how to bring up skiing without hurting Alex's feelings," Jenna added. "Or Abby's, or Priya's."

"It's like we've all been walking around on eggshells," Nat said. "It stinks."

Tori sniffled. "I wonder what the girls in New York are doing today. I bet they don't have awful weather like this. I miss them." She sighed. "If you guys want to fly home tomorrow instead of Monday, that's okay with me."

"What?" Alyssa said. "You planned this incredible weekend for us and there's no way we're skipping out on you." The other girls echoed the same feeling.

"I think Grace already caught her next flight home," Tori said. "Where is she, anyway?"

Nat glanced toward the bathrooms, but then she heard a familiar voice crackle to life on the stage speakers.

"We're dedicating this song to all of our Camp Lakeview friends from Bunks 4A and 4C. Even though we're not in the same place tonight, we still share the same spirit."

"Omigod," Nat squealed, grabbing Tori's arm. "Look! It's Grace!"

The beginning chords to "We Are Family" thrummed through the speakers, and the spotlight shone down on Grace. She was wearing a huge grin as she grabbed the mike with *American Idol* finesse.

"Is that her cell phone she's holding up to the mike?" Tori asked, giggling a little even as she wiped a few lingering tears from her eyes.

"Yup," Jenna said, laughing.

Just then, Grace launched into song. *"We are family, all my Lakeview sisters and me."*

But there was another voice singing along with her into the mike—a voice that Nat recognized right away. "That's *Brynn* singing with Grace! Grace must have called her in New York from the bathroom."

Nat gave Tori a hug. "See, girl? Everything's going to be just fine . . . between all of us."

"We are family," Grace and Brynn belted out. *"Get up everybody and sing."* Grace sashayed out into the audience and over to the girls' booth, where she grabbed Tori's hand and pulled her to her feet.

"Come on, guys!" Brynn's voice shouted from Grace's cell phone. "I want you on your feet and singing with us."

Nat formed a conga line with Jenna, Alyssa, and Tori, and the four of them followed Grace onto the stage where they linked arms, dancing and singing to the music.

"Everyone can see we're together, as we walk on by," Nat chimed in, singing with Tori and the other girls. And for the first time all day, she saw Tori break into a genuine, relaxed smile.

As they wrapped up the song, the audience burst into loud applause, and Jenna launched into a Lakeview cheer, with Brynn, Grace, and the other girls joining in. When they finally sat down at their table to catch their breath, Grace put her cell phone in the center of the table so that they could all hear Brynn.

"Thanks for the backup vocals," Grace said to

her. "Where are you, anyway?"

"I'm at this restaurant—Jekyll and Hyde—with everyone else. Luckily, it's loud in here, so no one really noticed me singing . . . I hope," Brynn said, laughing.

"I was worried you wouldn't pick up when I called. We weren't sure if you guys would want to hear from us this weekend."

"Actually," Brynn said, "we were just about to call you guys, too!"

"Wow," Alyssa said, smiling. "See, even though things are weird, we're all still on the same wavelength. How cool is that?"

"This whole thing has been so stupid," Brynn said, "and tonight we decided that it wasn't worth messing up our friendships anymore. Besides, we miss you guys!"

"We miss you, too!" Tori said. "I'm sorry we couldn't all be together this weekend."

"And *I'm* really sorry I forgot to ask you about your audition," Grace told Brynn. "I feel awful that I didn't know you played Eliza. That's amazing!"

"Well, my parents filmed the play, so I can still mail you guys all a copy of the DVD they made."

"Great!" Nat said. "And we'll send you some pics of the mountains here."

"And some of Nat falling down the ski slopes," Jenna teased.

"Watch it." Nat glared at Jenna jokingly.

"Well, Nat," Brynn said. "You might not be great at skiing, but I *know* you're great at boy advice. And I'm in desperate need of some of that right now."

"I have to warn you," Nat said, "I'm having some boy troubles myself, but I'll try."

"It's about Jordan," Brynn started.

As she listened to Brynn, Nat looked around the table at the happy faces of her friends. For a split second, she forgot that they were three thousand miles away from the girls at the reunion. She had no idea how Grace had done it, but somehow, she had started to bring the Lakeview girls back together again. And just like that, what had began as a dreary day turned into great one. It felt like camp all over again.

Even though talking to Nat about the whole Jordan sitch did make Brynn feel a little bit better (and the karaoke had helped, too), it was obvious that none of the girls—not even Nat or Tori—could come up with a good explanation for why he was a no-show. But just the fact that all the girls were talking again lifted Brynn's spirits. And so did the fun atmosphere at Jekyll & Hyde.

The whole place was set up like a haunted mansion, with skeletons and mummies hanging from the center of the room and dangling from dark corners. Black-and-white horror movies played on televisions hanging from the ceiling, and creepy music oozed from the corner where a skeleton in a tux sat playing an ancient, dust-covered organ. Dr. Steve had reserved a special section of the restaurant just for Lakeview, overlooking Dr. Jekyll's laboratory. Flickering orange candles lit up the lab where an animated model of

Frankenstein was strapped to a long table, struggling to free himself. It was all so much fun that Brynn couldn't help but feel cheered.

While she ate her Mummy Burger, she put the girls in Tahoe on speakerphone so that Alex, Abby, Sarah, and the other girls could say hi. Once everyone started talking, the floodgates opened up. Nat wanted to hear every detail about *Stomp!*; Sarah and Abby wanted to know what the scenery was like in Tahoe; Jenna wanted to tease Alex about Adam; and Tori wanted to apologize to everyone one more time for not being able to invite all the girls on the ski trip.

"Hey," Jenna said, "I'm going to send a picture of us to Brynn's cell right now."

Valerie, Priya, Chelsea, Abby, and the rest of the girls crowded around Brynn's cell phone as a picture popped up of Nat, Tori, Alyssa, Jenna, and Grace grinning and making faces from their table at the Overlook. And Sarah snapped a picture of Brynn and the other girls holding up their glasses of Dr. Jekyll's elixir to send to Grace's phone in Tahoe.

As the girls talked, Dr. Jekyll himself came onstage and announced a big round of applause for the Lakeview Campers, and then asked for volunteers to participate in one of Dr. Jekyll's "experiments."

Brynn didn't even notice Abby and Sarah pointing to her until Dr. Jekyll said, "Would the girl with the lovely singing voice at Lakeview table four please come to the stage! We heard her performance of 'We Are Family' a few minutes ago, and now we'd love for her to do a duet of the 'Monster Mash' with our very own mystery guest, Tobias Werewolf."

Alex nudged her. "Hey, Brynn, that's you."

"Get up there, girl!" Abby said, whistling and clapping for her.

"No way! I already embarrassed myself with the karaoke and I am *not* going up there!" But Abby, Sarah, Adam, and David were already pulling her out of her seat.

Reluctantly, Brynn took the stage with Dr. Jekyll while the rest of the Lakeview campers broke into earsplitting cheers.

"You have to look the part first," Dr. Jekyll said, handing her a lab coat, glasses, and a poofy mad scientist wig to wear. Brynn put them on, and when she did, she could feel herself putting on her best drama face, too.

"And now, here comes Tobias, your duet partner," Dr. Jekyll said. "He told us he traveled all the way from Transylvania to see you tonight. And boy, let me tell you, he can howl with the best of them."

The spotlight shone down on a werewolf who walked over to Brynn and—to her surprise—pulled a dozen red roses from behind his back.

"For me?" Brynn asked in confusion, and the werewolf nodded his shaggy head. It was the last thing she would've expected, but she took the roses as the "Monster Mash" began, and then danced the entire song with the werewolf by her side. When the song finally finished, Brynn was blushing and breathless, but smiling. What happened next, though, surprised her even more than the roses had. The werewolf clasped her hand between his paws and bent to kiss it.

"Thanks to both of our 'Monster Mash' dancers," Dr. Jekyll said, handing them each a Jekyll & Hyde Club T-shirt. "We hope you'll come back to visit us again soon."

Brynn stepped off the stage, but just as she was about to sit back down, the werewolf tapped her on the shoulder. Then he slowly pulled off his werewolf headpiece, and Brynn gasped. There was Jordan, looking tired and disheveled, and giving her a very sheepish smile.

"Hi," he said quietly as the Lakeview Campers broke into deafening cheers. He glanced over Brynn's shoulder at their friends, who were hooting and hollering even louder than before. "Do you think we could talk for a minute . . . alone?"

Brynn nodded, still not quite believing her boyfriend was here (wearing a werewolf costume to boot) and followed him to a quieter hallway near the bathrooms.

"I didn't think you'd come," Brynn said, not sure whether she was angry, worried, relieved, or just plain confused to see him. "And I definitely didn't expect to see you wearing *that*."

"I only just flew in a couple of hours ago," Jordan said. "And I wanted to surprise you, so when I got here I volunteered to dress up like this for the 'Monster Mash.' Kenny, Adam, and David helped rig it all beforehand. I was hoping it'd keep you from yelling at me for at least a few minutes." He smiled. "Brynn, I'm so sorry I missed your show, and for not being able to call you this week." He motioned to the roses. "I hope those'll make up for the ones I was planning to give you on your opening night. But I don't blame you if you really hate me."

"Thanks for the roses," Brynn said, cradling them in her arms. "And no, I don't hate you." She paused and took a deep breath. "But I would like to know why you didn't come, and why you didn't call."

Jordan kept his eyes on the ground. "Last Saturday, on the morning of your opening show, my parents found out that my grandpa had had a really bad heart attack. We had to fly down to Florida right away, and I didn't have time to call you before I left. I was going to call from Florida, but we left in such a hurry that I forgot my cell phone. And without my cell phone I didn't have your number. Priya was out of town, so I couldn't get your number from her, and I tried information once, but your number's not listed. My parents are still down in Florida, but they agreed to let me fly straight into JFK tonight so I could come to the reunion."

Brynn cautiously took Jordan's hand, er, paw. She wasn't used to being so forward, but Jordan looked so sad and stressed, she knew it was the right thing to do. "That's awful," she said. "How's your grandpa doing now?"

"He's still in critical condition," Jordan said, "but the doctors say he's getting stronger every day, and that he stands a good chance of recovering."

"That's great," Brynn said.

Jordan nodded. "But I'm really, really sorry I

couldn't call. And my grandpa doesn't have a computer in his house, so I couldn't e-mail you, either."

"Hey," Brynn said. "I'm not mad anymore."

"Really?" Relief flooded his face.

"Really. You had an important reason for not coming to the show. I just hope your grandpa gets better soon."

"Thanks for understanding," Jordan said. "That means a lot to me."

"Sure," Brynn said. "I feel so much better now that I know what happened. And you can always come see my next play. I'm planning on trying out for *The Music Man* in a few weeks."

"I'll make sure I don't miss another one again." Jordan smiled. Then, before Brynn knew exactly what was happening, he gave her a quick peck on the cheek.

"You're the best, Brynn," he said.

Brynn leaned against the wall, trying to catch her breath. But then David whistled from the booth. "Hey, Jordan, are you going to continue your reunion romance or eat your food? Because if you don't, I will."

"Don't even think about it," Jordan said. "We're coming in a minute."

"Ooh la la," Priya started teasing then, eyeing Brynn's roses. "There must be a full moon tonight."

"Watch it," Jordan said, growling playfully. "Werewolves have a mean bite. And speaking of werewolves, I think it's time I retired Tobias." He scratched his neck. "This thing weighs a ton, and it's giving me hives."

Brynn laughed. "Well, when you're done transforming back into human form, come have some fried bat wings at our table."

As Jordan disappeared into the bathroom to change out of the costume and return it to Dr. Jekyll, Brynn headed back to her table, where she quickly filled the girls in on everything that had happened. Sarah had already sent Tori and the other Tahoe girls a pic of Brynn and Jordan's duet, and then Tori sent them a clip of Jenna belting out "Karma Chameleon." When Jordan sat down next to Brynn, she beamed at him and then glanced down at her mood ring, which was shimmering a bright blue for happiness, just like she'd guessed it would be.

After dinner finished up, it was time for everyone to go their separate ways. Brynn hugged Jordan good-bye, and he promised to call her first thing next week to plan another date soon. After Alex and Sarah said good-bye to Adam and David, all the girls headed back to the hotel with the counselors. Even though it was almost eleven o'clock by the time they got back, nobody was tired. Andie pulled out *Cosmo Girl*, and pretty soon Brynn and the rest of the girls were crowded into her room in their pj's to take some romance quizzes and find out their horoscopes. Then, Brynn, Abby, Alex, and Sarah stayed up way past midnight talking, laughing, and pigging out on the stash of candy Andie had given them earlier in the day.

When Brynn finally crawled into bed, she couldn't stop smiling. Yesterday afternoon, she hadn't been sure she'd have any fun at the reunion, especially if she didn't hear from Jordan. But the weekend was turning out much better than she'd ever expected. She'd figured things out with Jordan, and the Lakeview girls were back on track. The rest of the weekend would be terrific, too, she was sure, but for now, it didn't get much better than this.

chapter
ELEVEN

Tori couldn't have asked for a better day for skiing if she'd tried. She smiled up at the crystal clear sky and the bright sun as she rushed down the slope. It was a beautiful Sunday morning, just cold enough to keep the fresh powder from turning slushy, but warm enough to keep the girls' hands and toes from freezing. And the day seemed even more perfect because, for the first time since she'd found out about the camp reunion, Tori was relaxed and amazingly happy.

It had been such a relief to get everything out in the open with the girls in New York last night, and now she didn't have to worry about whether Nat, Alyssa, Grace, and Jenna were having a good time with her in Tahoe. She could tell, just by their easy smiles and nonstop chatter, that the girls were back to normal with each other, and with her.

She swiveled her body to pull to a stop midway down the slope and wait for the other girls, but when she turned, she saw Jenna was right on her heels. She'd mastered snowplowing this morning in their lesson with Heidi, and now she was already parallel skiing and using her poles like a pro.

"Avalanche!" Jenna cried, sliding sideways the last few feet to send a huge wave of powder crashing over Tori.

"This means war," Tori sputtered through her laughter as she wiped the snow off her face. She used her poles to pop the bindings on Jenna's skis, and Jenna's boots flew out from under her, sending her crashing onto the packed snow. As the grand finale, Alyssa and Grace used their skis to send their own tidal waves of snow over Jenna.

"Okay, okay. I surrender!" Jenna laughed breathlessly.

Tori whipped out her cell phone and snapped a picture. Last night, all the 4A and 4C girls had made a pact to keep in constant touch for the rest of the weekend, and it was already working. Alex had sent them a short video this morning of Chelsea snoring away as Priya and Sarah covered her hair with shaving cream. "Since Jenna's not here," Alex had text-messaged, "we decided to do one eensy-weensy prank in her honor." And Valerie had taken some snapshots of the girls devouring massive Reuben sandwiches for lunch at the Carnegie Deli in Times Square.

"What a great candid for the girls back East," Tori said, checking out her shot of Jenna covered in snow. "What do you always say, Lyss? A picture's worth a thousand words?"

"You got it," Alyssa said, rubbing a little more snow into Jenna's hair before Jenna wrestled her down onto the snow, too. Grace was nearly doubled over laughing, but when Tori looked for Nat, she saw her standing a few feet away, pale and frowning, her cell phone to her ear.

"What's wrong?" Tori asked, and the other girls stopped fooling around when they saw Nat's serious face, too.

"Simon called a little while ago," she said, hitting the speaker on her phone so they could all listen to his message:

"Hey, Nat. I missed you at the reunion yesterday. We had so much fun, but it would've been great to have you there, too. The guys and I are taking the train into the city from Blake's place right now. We're going to play paintball at Chelsea Piers, so I thought I'd call now before we get too busy. I guess if I don't talk to you before then, I'll see you tomorrow after your flight. Um . . . there's something I wanted to talk to you about, so it'll be good to see you face-to-face . . . finally. Bye."

"That's not so awful," Alyssa said. "You need to talk to him, too, right? Wasn't that your plan?"

Nat nodded miserably. "But what if he's going to tell me he . . . you know . . . loves me, or something? And then I go and break his heart by telling him our long-distance dating thing isn't working?"

Tori's mouth dropped. "Is that what you're going to tell him?"

Nat swallowed and took a deep breath. "I think so. I'm really not happy with the way things are right now, and it wouldn't be fair to hold off on telling him that any longer."

"That's major," Jenna said. "I never thought you

guys would break up."

"I don't really want to break up yet," Nat said. "It's more like I want us both to relax and spend time with our friends, and not worry so much about getting together for dates and stuff. Then, whatever happens, happens."

Alyssa put her arm around Nat. "It's good that you're going to get it all out in the open."

"Yeah," Nat said, "but how am I going to say it without passing out and without breaking his heart?"

"Hey, you didn't faint the first time you saw mess-hall food, did you?" Jenna teased. "So you'll be fine."

"And give Simon a little credit," Alyssa said. "He might handle it better than you think. I bet you he's worrying about a lot of the same things you are."

"You could always try doing what I do when I'm in an embarrassing situation," Grace said. "I just pretend I'm playing a role on stage, and that it's not really me who just tripped going up the stairs, or who spilled milk all over the cutest guy in school. Everything is easier to do when you're in character."

"You can do it," Tori said, hugging Nat. "If you're brave enough to try skiing for the first time in a blizzard, you can definitely handle a talk with Simon."

"I hope so," Nat said, just as Tori's cell rang. "Omigod, if that's Simon looking for me, tell him I bit it on a black diamond." She pushed off the snow and started downhill, wobbling unsteadily as she went.

"Hey, Sarah!" Tori said into the phone. She tried to wave to Nat to stop, but Nat was already halfway down the slope. "Did you get the pictures I just sent?"

"Yup." Sarah laughed. "Jenna looked like a snowman after a bad hair day. None of us can stop laughing."

"She'd better not be laughing at me," Jenna whispered to Tori.

"Never," Tori whispered to her. But when she saw Nat tumbling downhill with skis and poles all a tangled blur, Tori said to Sarah, "Um . . . I'd better go before Nat skis off the side of the mountain or breaks a limb."

She hung up after promising to call New York again later, and then skied over to help Nat to her feet.

"I think I'm getting the hang of it," Nat said optimistically. "Maybe all I needed was a little panic to motivate me. I might even be able to tackle some mole hills someday."

"I think you mean moguls," Alyssa laughed. "But way to think positively."

"Last one down is a rotten egg," Nat cried, taking off again.

Tori giggled and started after her with the other girls following. As she raced through the snow, she started singing the Lakeview alma mater at the top of her lungs, and the other four girls joined in. As she sang and laughed with her friends, Tori thought that the only thing that could possibly make this day any more perfect would be to have all the Lakeview campers together, just like last summer. But for now, this came in a close second.

Sarah leaned back against the velvet seat of the carriage and smiled as she listened to the happy clip-clop of the horses' hooves on the pavement. Sunday afternoon was cold but sunny, and there were patches of snow still on the lawns in Central Park, but even the bare trees were a pretty sight. After she and the other girls had slept in late this morning, Andie and Mia had had the great idea to take them to the Carnegie Deli for lunch and then for a carriage ride through Central Park. With the city looking postcard-worthy in the bright winter light and her friends by her side, Sarah felt like she was in the middle of a Norman Rockwell painting.

"We are such ladies of luxury today," she said, grinning at Alex, Brynn, and Abby, who were all seated in the horse-drawn carriage with her, wrapped under a cozy fleece blanket.

"Yeah," Brynn said, "now all we need is a penthouse overlooking the park and we'd be set." She sighed dreamily. "And it would have been nice to have the guys along for this ride, too. How romantic!"

Alex giggled. "Yeah, I'd like to see Adam and David give up paintball to go for a carriage ride. That'd *never* happen. They're probably covered in paint like some warped rendition of *Lord of the Flies* right now." She nudged Brynn. "I bet Jordan would've come along for this ride, though."

"Yeah, Brynn," Sarah said, watching her turn red. "I think he would've done anything to keep you happy this weekend. And you haven't stopped smiling since you guys made up. Are you sure you didn't have any of Dr. Jekyll's love potion last night?"

"Look who's talking," Brynn teased. "I think I saw you holding hands with David last night, too."

Now it was Sarah's turn to blush. "Only for a few minutes," she said, to which everyone laughed. Sarah looked over at Valerie, Priya, Chelsea, and Karen, who were riding in a second carriage next to them, with the counselors in a third behind them.

"Kodak moment!" she said, waving to the girls in the other carriage. "Say 'Big Apple'!" She snapped a picture of them with their arms wrapped around one another, and then took one of her carriage and one of the counselors'. "I'm going to send these to Nat and Tori's cells right now."

Less than a minute after Sarah sent the pictures, her cell rang. "Hi, Nat!" she said, clicking on speakerphone so that all the girls could talk.

"We just got the pictures. You guys look like you're living the high life in the city. Riding in carriages, ice-skating in Central Park. It's a little touristy," Nat teased, "but since you don't have a native city slicker such as myself to show you the ropes this time, I guess you're doing okay."

"Hey, you can't blame us for being sucked into New York tourism," Abby said. "A horse and carriage is just way too good to pass up."

Nat laughed. "That's okay, we're doing our fair share of touristy things here, too. We're at the snow tubing park right now. See?"

A video clip of Jenna and Alyssa sliding down a hill in a huge inner tube flashed across Sarah's screen. "Awesome!" Sarah said, giggling with Abby as she watched the inner tube collide with Tori and Grace's.

"Yeah," Nat said. "I've discovered that crash landing is much better in an inner tube than on skis. You don't have as far to fall."

"When do you guys fly back?" Brynn asked.

"Tomorrow morning," Nat said, "but we don't land back East until the afternoon."

"We're leaving tomorrow afternoon, too," Alex said. "We're going to the butterfly exhibit at the Museum of Natural History later today, and then to the ballet tonight at Lincoln Center. And tomorrow morning we're going shopping in the East Village."

"Hey guys, it's me, Tori. I just heard the magic word, 'shopping.' I want to hear all about it so that whenever I get out to New York I can hit all the cool consignment shops you find."

While the other girls talked, Sarah went quiet at the thought of having to leave all of her friends tomorrow. She'd probably see a few of them before camp started again, but summer still seemed like a long way away. And since she hadn't gotten to see Jenna, Nat, Tori, Grace, or Alyssa at all at the reunion, it would be even longer since she saw them.

"We miss you guys," she said, "but at least on this trip we didn't have to worry about Jenna raiding our candy stash in the middle of the night, or sticking our hands in ice water while we were sleeping . . ."

"Actually," Abby admitted, "I even sort of

missed her pranks."

"Really?" piped up Jenna in the background, sounding delighted. "In that case, I'll have some ready and waiting for you on the first day of camp."

"Jenna!" everyone cried at the same time, and then broke into giggles.

"I took a lot of pictures with my digital camera this weekend," Nat said. "I'll e-mail them to you guys next week."

"Great!" Sarah said. "We'll send the ones we took, too."

After they hung up, Brynn said, "You know, I never thought I'd be saying this, because I really did want to go on that ski trip with Grace and the other girls. But now I'm actually glad I didn't get invited to go. Because I wouldn't have missed out on this weekend with you guys for anything."

"Me neither," Sarah said, smiling. "But next year we have to make sure we're all here, no matter what. We'll have to break into Dr. Steve's secret camp files to find out the date of the next camp reunion so there's no chance of us double-booking two things in the same weekend ever again. Lakeview get-togethers just aren't the same without all of the Lakeview campers."

"Do you wish you'd gone to Tahoe instead of the reunion?" Abby asked, looking at Sarah with a seriousness she rarely had.

"No way," Sarah said. "I wouldn't have had much fun in Tahoe anyway, without you. Where you go, I go."

"So," Abby said, "do you still want to give skiing a

try? I could see if my parents can take us up to Vermont for a weekend before the season's over."

"That would be great!" Sarah said, her mind already spinning with possibilities. "Of course, I returned the ski jacket I bought, and it's going to take me into the next century to pay my mom back for the Tahoe ticket I canceled. But somebody at school might have ski stuff we can borrow for the weekend."

"I'll talk to my parents about it this week," Abby said.

"Great!" Sarah said. "Of course, you know I'm going to smoke you on the slopes, but as long as you're okay with that . . ."

"Ha. I think you mean *I'm* going to smoke *you*," Abby said.

"We'll see about that," Sarah teased.

As the carriage slowed to a stop, Sarah clicked one final picture and stepped onto the sidewalk.

"Come on," she said, wrapping her arms around her friends. "This weekend's not over yet, and we owe it to the girls in Tahoe to pack in as much as we can, so let's go."

chapter

TWELVE

As Nat looked up at the Manhattan skyscrapers through the window of her cab, she let out a little sigh. It was good to be coming home to the city she loved, but saying good-bye to the other girls earlier this morning had left her feeling sad, too. Now, as the cab pulled up in front of her apartment building, all she wanted to do was unpack, slip into her comfiest yoga pants, and log onto the camp blog to talk to everyone.

The last thing she expected to see when she stepped out of the cab was Simon. But there he was, sitting on a bench near the front entrance of her apartment building, obviously waiting for her. What was he doing here? She'd said that she would call him once she landed, and that they'd pick a time to meet before he headed back to Connecticut tonight. But it was only three in the afternoon. She wished she could dive into the cab and have the driver take her around the block a few times, at least until she figured out how to plan the talk she needed to have with him. But then Simon glanced up and spotted her, and Nat knew it was too late for stall tactics.

"Nat!" Simon rushed over to her, but when he

got within a few feet, instead of giving her a hug like he normally would have, he stopped short, hesitating. "I know I probably should've called you first, but I checked with your mom earlier, and she said your flight was on time, so I figured I'd just stop by your place and wait." He brushed a hand through his hair nervously. "I hope that's okay."

"Sure," Nat said. But she wasn't sure . . . not of anything. As she paid the cab driver and collected her bags, her stomach churned uncomfortably, and she knew it wasn't jetlag causing it. "Um, were you waiting long?"

"No, only about twenty minutes." He swooped down to grab her suitcase and carry-on from her hands. "I'll get these."

"Thanks," Nat said, leading the way into her building. They rode up the elevator in silence, while Nat tried to think of what to tell her mom about Simon's surprise visit. Simon, too, seemed lost in his own thoughts.

"Mom!" Nat called out when she opened the door. "Guess who's here?"

"Um, let me see," her mom called from the kitchen. "My estranged daughter turned ski pro?" But when she stepped into the living room, there was no disguising her surprise. "Oh, Simon! How nice to see you! I thought you and Nat were going to see each other a little later on today."

Simon blushed. "Well, I . . ."

"He wanted to surprise me," Nat interjected, hoping to stop any of her mom's questions before they started. "Is it okay if we hang out in my room for a little while?"

Her mom nodded. "Sure, hon. I'm just putting together a snack for myself, so I'll bring some in to you guys in a few minutes, too."

"Great," Nat said, trying her best to fake like everything was okay, but she was pretty sure her mom was picking up on the weirdness of this whole situation, too.

Once she and Simon were safely in her room, Nat took a deep breath and sat down at her desk. It was better to start this now, and get it over with, hard as it would be.

"Simon," she began, "thanks for stopping by. I know you're probably missing out on some stuff with Blake and the other guys to be here." Her heart knocked around like crazy. "There was something I wanted to talk to you about . . ."

"Me too," Simon jumped in, perching himself nervously on the very edge of her bed. "I've been thinking . . ." He sucked in a ragged breath. "I know we've been dating for a while and everything, but lately I've been feeling like . . ."

He paused, and Nat closed her eyes, dreading the L-word that she was sure was coming next.

"Like this long-distance thing is just too much pressure. For both of us."

"What?" Nat blinked. Well, this was a shocker.

"Yeah." Simon gulped, then rushed on. "I've felt like lately you might have been a little . . . frustrated that we weren't seeing each other that much. And I know you have tons of friends here in the city. And I'm super busy with my friends up in Connecticut, too. And I guess I just want us to slow down and just have some fun, without worrying about this whole dating thing so much." He dug his shoe into the carpet and stared out the window.

"I can't believe this," Nat said.

"I know. I hope you won't be too mad at me, but I think it's the best thing to do. 'Cause your friendship means a lot to me, and I don't want to mess that up with too much serious stuff." He stopped and chanced a look at Nat.

Nat took a deep breath, and then . . . she smiled. "Simon," she said, "I'm not mad at you. I'm actually totally relieved. This is crazy, but I was going to tell you the same exact thing tonight. I've been worrying about it for weeks. I didn't know how to talk to you about it, because I was afraid of hurting your feelings."

Simon gave a small laugh. "Really? So you're okay with this?"

"More than okay," Nat said. "I want us to stay great friends, too. And whatever happens down the road, or doesn't happen, will be fine."

"Wow," Simon said. "This is great. I was so afraid you'd hate me."

"Nope," Nat laughed. "Not a chance. I'm just so glad we're going to stay friends."

"Me too," Simon said. "Hey, I didn't even ask you how your trip was!"

"It was great," Nat said, "but I'm sorry I missed out on the reunion. I have lots to tell you about Tahoe, though." And suddenly, she knew it was true. In the last few weeks, she'd dreaded talking to Simon, not knowing what to say to him. But now, it was like the dam had broken and she couldn't wait to tell him everything, just like it used to be when they were first starting to become friends. "Hey, I have an idea. My mom's probably making some tofu snack for us, but do you want to go grab a slice of authentic, thin crust New York pizza from the place around the corner? I can tell you all about the ski trip, and you can tell me all about the reunion."

"Pizza or tofu," Simon said. "It's not even a question. Pizza all the way."

"I hear you." Nat grabbed her coat and told her mom where they were going. As they stepped back out onto the bustling city sidewalk filled with Presidents' Day tourists, Nat broke into a huge grin. She had a feeling that everything between her and Simon was going to be just fine. It was the start of a whole new type of friendship for the two of them, and with any luck, they'd be closer than ever before. The ski trip had helped clear her head, and now she was ready to face the spring and the summer and all the new adventures waiting for her. And she couldn't wait to IM the girls tonight and tell them all about it.

△ △ △

That evening, Brynn double-checked the train schedule on the board at Penn Station one more time, and sighed when she saw her boarding gate pop up.

"That's me," she said, turning to rest of the girls,

who were all waiting for trains to take them home, too. This was the moment she'd been dreading since yesterday, knowing it would probably be months before she'd see her friends again. After such an amazing weekend, it was hard to face the idea of heading back to school tomorrow, and even worse, going back home knowing how long it would be before camp started up again. She tried to muster up a smile, but she still felt a little teary-eyed, too.

"All right, sweetie," Andie said, handing Brynn her weekend bag. "Call me on my cell when you get home just to let me know you're okay. You know how much Dr. Steve loves his head counts, and every camper has to be accounted for tonight."

"I'll call," Brynn said, then to Alex, Sarah, Abby, Priya, Val, and the other girls, she added, "And I'll IM you guys tonight, too. I'm going to post my pics on our camp blog as soon as I get home." She giggled. "Alex, I think I got a great one of you catching Adam when he started to fall at the ice-skating rink."

Alex laughed. "I'm sure Adam will *really* appreciate that photo going public."

"And I got one of you and Jordan holding hands," Priya said, winking at Brynn. "My two favorite *lurve*-birds."

"Yeah, yeah," Brynn teased. "Just wait until I get ahold of a picture of you and that Riley guy . . . forget the camp blog, I'm going to send it in to *Us Weekly*."

"Um, considering that the only person who's less of a somebody than me is Riley, I'm not too concerned about *Us Weekly* wanting my pictures." Priya laughed. "But with your budding acting career, I really would keep an eye out for the paparazzi. Which reminds me, if you get the part in *The Music Man*, count me in for a ticket."

"Me too," Valerie said.

"It's only a few hours on the train from Boston to Jersey," Sarah added.

Abby nodded. "We wouldn't miss it."

"And you know I'm your biggest fan," said Alex.

"We'll come, too," Andie said, gesturing to Mia, Becky, and Sophie. "It'll be like a mini reunion."

"Yeah," Brynn said, loving the idea. "And maybe Grace, Nat, Alyssa, and Jenna can come, too. Tori won't be able to, but we can send her a DVD of it."

"So now you *have* to get the part," Alex said. "How else will we get to see one another before camp?"

"I'll see what I can do," Brynn said. She'd brought the script along with her in her weekend bag, but she hadn't had a chance to look at it yet. But now, she was eager to dive right into it. It would be perfect reading material for her train ride home. Just knowing that her friends would all come to the play would make her try even harder for the part.

The station's intercom clicked on just then, announcing final boarding for Brynn's train, and Andie said, "You'd better go. I don't want to have to tell Dr. Steve that you missed your train."

"Okay," Brynn said, and she gave each of her

friends a huge hug. "We'll see one another soon."

"And we'll e-mail and IM all the time," Sarah said.

"Yeah," Abby joined in. "It'll be like we're not even apart. You'll see."

Brynn waved to her friends as she took the escalator down to the platform, and even after they'd disappeared from view, she kept seeing their faces in her mind as she boarded the train. She checked her cell phone as she sat down, and had two messages waiting. One was from Jordan.

"I just got home a few minutes ago," he said. "My grandpa's going home from the hospital next week, so he's doing much better. Thanks for being so understanding about everything. I, um . . . I miss you. Give me a call later."

Brynn blushed. He'd actually said he missed her. That was *huge*. And she realized that she really liked the idea of being missed by him. But hopefully now that things had settled down with his grandpa, they wouldn't have to wait too long before they saw each other again.

The second message was a text note from Nat. Nat had sent it to Brynn's cell, and also to all the other girls from 4A and 4C. "Hi, girls," Nat had written. "Let's conf call 2nite . . . 8 P.M.! I have big news about Simon. Can't wait to tell u all about it. TTYL."

Brynn smiled. The Lakeview girls might not live in the same place, but they shared the same spirit, and it was great to have everyone back together again. It was almost like they'd never be apart . . . not really.

Even though the weekend was finally over, she'd go home with a lot of great memories of the reunion, of holding hands with Jordan under the twinkling lights of Manhattan's skyline, and of filling up on great food, friendship, and fun. And this was just the beginning. She would have a great time over the next few months, waiting for warm weather to come again, and wondering what the summer would bring.

Turn the page for a sneak preview of

camp CONFIDENTIAL

A Fair to Remember

available soon!

chapter

Posted by: Jenna
Subject: Memorial Day fun!!!

Hey there, peeps of 4A and 4C, have I got a surprise for you! This Memorial Day weekend my father has offered to take us all up to the family's lake house so we can pig out, stay up all night talking, and make up for lost reunion time. Ladies . . . pack your bags! I mean, even though the reunion weekend turned out all right in the end, we *WERE* split up. And that, we all agreed, was no good. I think it's about time we got back together for a little two-bunk bonding, don't you? Plus, Memorial Day at the lake is out of control. They do this whole old-fashioned weekend-long picnic/carnival thing with tons of food and rides and tons of food and shows and tons of food and fireworks.

Did I mention the *TONS of FOOD*?

(You know how much I love my stomach.)

Anyway, the point is, you are all invited and I hope to see each and every one of you there. And for those of you who are wondering (and I know you're out there), no, this is not one of my practical jokes. I can see why you would think so, but I'd never joke about a thing like this.

I am perfectly and totally serious. But if you really need to confirm, you can have your parents call my dad. He's totally willing to answer any questions.

So pack your bags, ladies! It's time to have the REAL reunion we've all been waiting for! Can't wait to see you!!!

▲ ▲ ▲

"Bathing suit . . . check!" Jenna Bloom sang to herself as she shoved her one-piece into her duffel bag. "Greenwood Lake sweatshirt . . . check! Baseball cap . . . check!"

She yanked open the drawer to her bedside table and considered her stash of practical joke paraphernalia. Should she bring the whoopee cushion? The foaming mouth gum? The skin cream that looked like it was from some chichi makeup counter, but in fact turned your skin green?

That could be fairly hilarious if she could convince Tori or Natalie that it was the latest in makeup technology from France or whatever.

But no. This weekend was not about pranks. It was about bonding with her friends. Being a "gracious hostess," as her mother had told her ten thousand times. And she had a feeling that Martha Stewart had never purposely turned her guests' faces green. With a deep breath and some serious willpower, Jenna slammed the drawer shut. No pranks this weekend.

This Memorial Day was going to be about good, clean fun.

"Jenna! Are you ready yet?" her mother called

up the stairs. "Your father is going to be here any minute!"

"I'm trying, Mom!" Jenna shouted back, shoving her flip-flops into the bag. "But this packing thing is complicated."

"Your brother was done an hour ago!" her mom called. "It's just three days!"

Jenna rolled her eyes and yanked her bag off the bed where it dropped to the floor with a thump. How could Adam have been done an hour ago? They had just gotten home from school around that time. It had taken Jenna a half hour just to locate her duffel bag and find herself three T-shirts that weren't covered in wrinkles.

But it made sense that her twin brother was all ready to go.

That was just the way he was. What Jenna couldn't figure out was why he wanted to go at all. Did he really want to spend the entire weekend in a house full of girls? How could that possibly be fun for him?

Well, at least we'll outnumber him eight to one, Jenna thought with a smirk, dropping down in front of her computer.

She had saved all the response e-mails from the friends who were coming to the lake and put them in their own little folder. On the list were Alex, Natalie, Grace, Brynn, Tori, Alyssa, and Valerie. Definitely a fun group. Jenna could not wait to see them all. She only wished that Sarah was able to come, but she had e-mailed a few days ago to decline. Apparently she had a big softball game that weekend that she just couldn't miss. Jenna understood that, being a sports fiend herself. Plus, this was Sarah's first year on her school team. She had tried out and made it after Abby, another camp friend who also went to Sarah's school, had talked her into it. Jenna was happy that Sarah was finally using her sick softball skills somewhere other than camp, but Sarah was going to be missed over the weekend.

"Jenna! Please finish up and come down!" Jenna's mother shouted. "Your father is going to want to hit the road as soon as he gets here."

"Just have to shut down my computer, Mom!" Jenna yelled back.

She quickly typed up an e-mail to Sarah.

To: SarahSports
From: Aries8
Subject: The Big Game

Hi Sarah!
Just wanted to wish you luck on your softball game this weekend! We'll be rooting for you from Greenwood Lake. Wish you could be there! We'll miss you!!!
Love,
Jenna

Jenna quickly logged off and shut down her computer. She heard her father's car pull up outside and her heart started to pound with excitement. This was it! The weekend was about to begin. In just a couple of hours she would be hanging out with all her friends.

With some effort, Jenna hoisted her heavy bag

from the floor and struggled through the door with it. She shut off her bedroom light and clambered down the stairs.

"He's here! He's here! He's here!" she cheered, jumping down the last few steps.

Her feet hit at an odd angle and she tripped forward, taking out a potted plant with her bag and tripping right into someone's chest.

"Easy there, killer," the victim said, steadying Jenna with his hands on her arms.

Okay. That was not a member of her family. Jenna stood up straight and looked right into the light green eyes of David Carson. David, Adam's friend from camp. David, Sarah's boyfriend. Jenna's heart took a nosedive and she stepped back. Practically jumped back.

"What are you doing here?" she blurted.

"Good to see you, too," David said with a smile. His floppy brown hair had been cut so that it didn't flop completely over his eyes anymore. It just sort of grazed his eyebrow. "And you're welcome."

"For what?" Jenna asked.

"For catching you," he said.

"I was fine, thanks," Jenna said, straightening her T-shirt.

"Yeah. Tell that to the wallpaper that almost rearranged your face," Adam said from behind her. "And David is here because Dad said I could bring a friend this weekend. You know, because you've got, like, four thousand of them coming."

Jenna whirled on her brother, whose curly

brown hair—so much like her own—was matted down by a Yankees baseball cap. "Maybe that's because this whole thing was my idea. You should have told me you were bringing someone."

"Why? So you could stick itching powder in his bed or something?" Adam asked, glancing out the window. He lifted his backpack as their dad started up the front walk. "I don't think so."

"No, I just . . . this whole weekend was my idea and . . .and . . . I would have wanted to know, that's all," Jenna said awkwardly, crossing her skinny arms over her chest.

"Well, now you do!" David told her with a smile.

Jenna narrowed her eyes at him. She just could not believe this was happening. Not just one boy on her perfect reunion weekend, but two. And why did it have to be this boy? The only boy she ever had a crush on? A totally humiliating crush that only ended when Jenna found out that he liked Sarah and Sarah liked him back. The two of them danced all night together at the camp social while Jenna looked on and tried not to be jealous. Now he was here and Sarah was not and the whole thing was just making her feel all hot in the face.

The doorbell rang and Adam rushed to respond. There stood their dad, a huge smile on his face, his sunglasses perched atop his head.

"Everyone ready for a fun weekend?" he asked, spreading his arms wide.

"Yeah!" Adam and David cheered, crowding out

the door.

Jenna yanked her bag up off the tile floor and sighed, following after the boy brigade. So much for her perfect weekend.

▲ ▲ ▲

Grace sat at the breakfast bar in her kitchen on Friday afternoon, eating her afternoon snack and staring at her history textbook.

She knew that she should be excited about her weekend at Greenwood Lake with her friends, but somehow she could just not get psyched with that big, ugly book laughing up at her. She took a sip of her milk and let out a huge, dramatic sigh.

"Something wrong, Grace?" her mother asked, turning off the water in the kitchen sink. She wiped her hands on a towel and walked over. "Shouldn't you be bouncing off the walls about now? Alyssa and her mom are going to be here to pick you up any second now."

"I know," Grace said, tucking a stray lock of her curly red hair behind her ear. "It's just . . . do I really have to bring . . . *that?*" she asked, throwing her hand out toward the thick book.

"Grace," her mother said in her stern, warning tone. "We've been over this and over this."

"I know," Grace said. "It's just this weekend is supposed to be fun. How am I going to have any fun if I have to study?"

Her mother stood up straight and sighed. She looked, as always, perfectly put together in a pair of light khakis and a plaid button-down shirt. Grace wondered if she'd ever look that perfect and pressed in her life.

"The only reason we're letting you go on this trip is because we have a deal. Don't tell me you're trying to back out of it. Because if you want to stay home . . ."

"No!" Grace blurted, suddenly on high alert. "No! I'll make good on the deal. Two hours of studying each day."

"Exactly," her mother said with a smile. "We only want you to pass that test on Tuesday. Because if you don't pass the test, you might not pass history for the year. And if you don't pass history for the year . . ."

"I know. I know. Summer school," Grace said, feeling heavy.

"And if you have to go to summer school . . ."

"It means I'll have to miss the first three weeks of camp," Grace finished. And that would be a nightmare. It would basically be the punishment to end all punishments. Grace could not miss out on camp. She only looked forward to it all year long from the moment she left her bunk for the last time in August until the moment she got back on the bus at the end of June. There was no way she could stay home from camp and study history instead.

Grace knew that she brought this upon herself. It was just that every time she opened her history textbook, something more important—and interesting—seemed to come up. Like IMs from her camp friends, or practice for the school play, or some great soap-opera marathon on cable.

She'd just always thought she would have the time to catch up, but now time had pretty much run out.

"But don't you think it's totally unfair to give a huge test the day after Memorial Day weekend?" Grace asked, getting up to put the bag of chocolate chip cookies back in the cupboard. "Come on, Mom. Even you have to admit that's evil."

Grace's mother hid a laugh behind her hand.

"Doesn't Mr. Joseph know that people have lives?" Grace added, throwing her hands out, hamming it up.

Her mother shook her head and smiled. "I'm sure your friends won't mind letting you alone for a few hours here and there this weekend," she said. "After all, they've always helped you study in the past. Like that summer when you had to catch up on your reading?"

Grace smiled. "Yeah. They were really great about that."

A horn tooted in the driveway and Grace's excitement finally kicked in. "They're here!" she cried, grabbing her mini suitcase and sleeping bag off the floor. "Bye, Mom!" she said, jumping up on her tiptoes to kiss her mother's cheek. She turned and ran for the door, yanking her denim jacket from the hook in the hallway along the way.

"Ahem!" Her mother cleared her throat loudly.

Grace stopped in her tracks and turned around. Her mom was standing a few feet behind her, holding her history textbook up in one hand.

Grace blushed.

"Oops! Don't know how I forgot that!" she joked, tromping back to her mother. She took the book in one arm and almost fell over from its weight. "That's only the most important thing for me to bring!" she said.

"Uh huh," her mother said with a smirk. She leaned down and kissed Grace on top of her red curls. "Have fun, honey. And study hard!"

"I will!" Grace said, running for the door again.

She rushed outside, closed the door behind her, and lifted her sleeping bag to wave awkwardly at the car. Alyssa waved back excitedly before jumping out of the backseat to help Grace with her things. Grace tucked her history book under her jacket as her friend ran up to her. The last thing she wanted to do was explain its presence to Alyssa. She wanted to forget all about the thing—for now.

"Hey, Grace!" Alyssa cried.

"Hey yourself!"

Alyssa looked amazing. She had grown out her dark brown hair to below her shoulders, and had worked one small braid into the front with a colorful ribbon woven through it. She wore a beaded tank top and long denim skirt, and her flip-flops had hand-painted flowers all over them.

"It's so good to see you!" Alyssa said, grabbing Grace up in a hug. Grace dropped her sleeping bag, and the book, of course, stabbed right into Alyssa's stomach through the jacket. "Ow," she said, rubbing at her tummy. "What was that?"

"Oh, nothing," Grace said. "Just a little light reading."

Alyssa looked at Grace like she was nuts, but didn't question her. "Let me get your bag. I'm dying to get up there already! We've been on the road ever since school let out. Sometimes I think South Jersey is just too far from everything."

"Except the shore," Grace pointed out.

Alyssa grinned. "Yes. I love that."

Grace smiled and picked up her sleeping bag again before following Alyssa back to her mom's station wagon. The book felt as if it was burning a hole through her New Jersey Devils T-shirt. She just couldn't imagine three whole days at Greenwood Lake with this thing taunting her the whole time, reminding her of what was at stake. Maybe she could "accidentally" drop it out the window somewhere along the drive.

Then she could actually have some fun this weekend.